DOCTOR WHO
AND THE TIME

DOCTOR WHO
AND THE
TIME WARRIOR

Based on the BBC television serial *The Time Warrior* by Robert Holmes by arrangement with the British Broadcasting Corporation

TERRANCE DICKS

TARGET

published by
the Paperback Division of
W. H. Allen & Co. Ltd

A Target Book

Published in 1978
by the Paperback Division of W. H. Allen & Co. Ltd
A Howard & Wyndham Company
44 Hill Street, London WIX 8LB

Text of book copyright © 1978 by Terrance Dicks
and Robert Holmes

'Doctor Who' series copyright © 1978 by the
British Broadcasting Corporation

Printed and Bound in Great Britain
by Richard Clay (The Chaucer Press) Ltd,
Bungay, Suffolk

ISBN 0 426 20023 3

Contents

Prologue

Linx was his name. He was a microsecond from obliteration.

A million miles out in the sterile black infinity his starship's sensors had warned him of the asteroid belt. His heavy, triple-digit hand moved just once and the starship, silent as a whisper in the night, curved in towards the very centre of the belt.

It was a tired, suicidal gamble.

An aeon had passed since his first sighting of the Rutan squadron. He had been making a fly-pass through the constellation of Sagittarius, where Rutan forces were reported to be massing, when the fighters had vectored on to him.

Linx was flying a reconnaissance ship, a lightly-armed V-class cruiser. He had turned for base, engaging spectronic drive and confident that he could out-run the fighters.

But they had stayed with him. Worse, they had out-manoeuvred him, cutting off every twist and turn, seeming to anticipate every feint and stratagem he had dredged up from his long career in the Space Corps.

The Rutan leader was an expert. Linx knew the difficulty of holding a squadron in combat formation. But all through the long chase the nine pursuit-ships had maintained their perfect parabola, never varying by a single degree, never offering the faintest hope of breaking past them.

Linx had waited. His ship matched the fighters in speed. They had no chance of coming within torpedo range. Normally, in such a situation, the pursuing force eventually broke off the chase.

In three galactic wars against the Rutans, as each side developed increasingly sophisticated sensors, Linx had grown accustomed to these inconclusive encounters.

Not so, apparently, in the Rutan leader's case. He held on with dogged persistency, forcing Linx's cruiser inexorably further and further out from the centre of the galaxy. They were already among the fringe systems when Linx, with chilled respect, suddenly appreciated the depths of the Rutan's strategy—saw how long ago the plan had formulated.

Soon he would be driven out even beyond the fringes of the galaxy. Out into the deep space of the intergalactic wastes. Out into the terrible regions where even light itself faded and died . . .

The vortex. The great ebb. They would finish him there. That was the chosen killing ground.

And the Rutan leader had seen it all in the first flashing instant of contact, seen his opening in the very second that Linx turned for home, seen, a thousand parsecs away, the inevitable end.

As his starship plunged into the great ebb and lost way, the Rutan fighters would stand off at a safe distance and launch their torpedoes. There could be no escape.

Then his sensors detected the asteroid belt.

Unchartable as icebergs, drifting forever through the dark inter-stellar void, the asteroids formed a ragged arc millions of miles across. Some—Linx knew—would be vast mountains of rock and iron and ice. Others were probably no bigger than a single grain of sand.

He sat now at the control module and watched his

8

detector screens. Nothing showed. Perhaps nothing would. With the cruiser in spectronic drive the scanners would barely pick up an approaching image before impact. At that speed even a single grain of sand striking the hull would have the effect of a fission shell. The cruiser would simply vanish.

Linx himself—the heavy bones, the flat powerful muscles, the leathery, hairless epidermis, the calculating brain . . . all that was Jingo Linx, Commander in the Sontaran Space Corps—would cease to exist. Instead, a million tiny globules of organic matter would be left floating like a giant puff ball in space.

A microsecond from obliteration . . .

Linx moved his hand again. The blood-stirring ineffably sweet strains of the Sontaran Anthem pulsed through the ship. Linx never took his eyes off the screens—little, red eyes that were like fire-lit caves under the great green-brown dome of a skull—but he felt a thrill of pride run through his body. He was a Sontaran and he was dying as a Sontaran should . . . throwing a challenge to the Rutans.

They would not follow him into the asteroid belt. They were cowards by nature. It was only because of their enormous natural resources that his people hadn't yet finally defeated them. In individual quality, in pride of arms, Sontarans were the rightful rulers of the galaxy and this time there would be no armistice; this time the war would be fought until the Rutan Empire— every last satellite—had been reduced to radioactive dust.

Nothing showed on the screens. Linx checked the panel readings. The cruiser was now more than halfway through the belt. And still there was nothing on the screens.

Almost for the first time since the fighters had locked

9

on, Linx felt a tiny glow of hope. Even if the Rutan leader was taking his squadron round the belt, his chances of making a second successful interception were mathematically negligible. If the cruiser passed through the belt unscathed he would at last be free to turn for base.

His home planet, Sontara, was on the further side of the galaxy. To reach it would entail a long voyage through largely hostile zones where he would need to maintain constant vigilance. Linx decided to take an energy burn while he had the opportunity.

He switched the deck monitor to active and un-clipped his feeder hose from the control module. Fumbling slightly, he connected the hose to the small vent behind his neck. On entry into the Space Corps all fliers underwent mechasurgery. A probic insertion in the trapezius enabled them to live as cyborgs, drawing energy from the burners that powered their starships.

It was just a small example of Sontaran technology, Linx thought loyally, allied to Sontaran will: the sub-limation of self to the greater end of military efficiency. Even so he hesitated before pressing the switch. He always dreaded taking a burn.

His hand moved on the switch and immediately the almost-pain came screaming up into his skull, bursting inside his brain in a searing silver convulsion. He had spoken with other fliers who claimed to be totally ob-livious throughout the period of a burn. If only it were so with him.

The flood of power through his tissues was like a roaring madness, a chaotic maelstrom of colour and sound depriving him of all sentient knowledge of the outside world. He felt himself clinging like a limpet within some solitary crevice of consciousness, aware only that he still existed . . . still existed . . . still . . .

The cruiser had cleared the asteroid belt by the time the auto-valve ended the burn. Linx came instantly awake, feeling wonderfully serene and composed. But, as always after a burn, he had an urge to remain connected to the feeder, free from the necessity of making decisions, drifting warmly in a gentle euphoria.

It was a dangerous urge and Linx forced himself to unclip the hose within moments of cut-off. He switched the deck monitor back to latent and keyed the astro-chart to lay course for Sontara. The course-pattern came up on his display panel almost immediately. Before relaying the pattern to the gyrotillers, however, Linx conducted a manual sweep with his scanners. It was a mandatory procedure before any change of course and he had no expectation—

He made a soft, bitter noise and stared in shock at the detector screens. Unbelievably, the Rutan squadron had followed him through the asteroid belt. The lean black darts of the pursuit ships formed a pattern of doom on his screens, seeming to stretch towards the cruiser like the talons of some giant claw.

The new energy drained from Linx's body. He felt a cold, despairing tiredness. No escape now. No chance of turning for Sontara. The gamble was finally lost.

All at once he noticed an apparent error on the display. There were nine ships in the Rutan squadron and only eight showed on the screen. Eight. There was only space where the port wing-leader should have been. The asteroid belt had claimed a victim.

Without pause for thought, Linx flung the cruiser towards the gap. The deck plates thrummed under his feet and he heard ice cracking from the hull as the ship twisted under torsional stresses far in excess of its design limits.

Then the starship was round and leaping forward

again. And behind him, on the detector screens, the Rutan fighters were swinging to follow. But now they were strung out, their formidable formation broken, and the Rutan leader, for the first time, had been a fraction late in responding. Perhaps he, too, was at last beginning to feel the strain.

The eighth and closest ship was holding its original course. Linx had expected that. The cruiser would cross its bows and for an infinitesimal but precisely calculable moment he would be vulnerable to its torpedoes.

On his screens the two tracks were converging fast. A red cross, projected by computer, pinpointed their exact intersection. The Rutan pilot, Linx knew, would be watching a similar display. Only on his screens there would be a second symbol, the small green circle of the firing activator. Theoretically, when the cross and the circle came together, the Rutan's torpedoes couldn't miss.

Linx switched on his port shields and then waited a little longer. Move too soon and the Rutan would have time to correct. He had to judge the move to a thousandth of a second, the very instant that the torpedoes streaked from their firing pads.

He had survived such encounters before; he was a space veteran. And so he sat coolly, tense but without anxiety, listening to his instinct and experience. The machinery and computers had played their part. Now it was flier against flier, Sontaran versus Rutan . . .

Linx moved. The circle and the cross had come together. He knew it as certainly as if he had been sitting on the Rutan control deck.

The cursitor heeled three degrees to port. The track shots on his screens flickered and adjusted. His own blip was central on the cross and now it was through, moving away, the two tracks no longer converging.

For a second he failed to recognise the alarm; it was so unexpected. And he had felt nothing. Not a tremor in the ship, not a single indication of damage. But already the control deck lights were fading.

Linx switched on the reserve circuits and hurriedly started a systems search. The deck monitor found the fault first.

'CVT check. Critical malfunction,' it whispered.

The Cyclo Vybe Transmitter was the heart of the ship. Even as Linx switched the monitor to component inspection its power register faded to zero.

'CVT check. Total malfunction,' the deck monitor reported.

Linx cancelled the inspection. It was pointless. The CV Transmitter had suffered a massive rupture. The Rutan fighter pilot, he realised, had played for safety, firing a bracket cluster in the hope of crippling the cruiser rather than aiming for a direct hit. And, ironically, his own evasive manoeuvre had turned the cruiser into the periphery of a burst.

Now, indeed, all hope had ended. The ship's speed was falling. It was only a matter of time—very little time —before the pursuing fighters overhauled him. All he could do now was to play the game to its finish.

A small solar system showed directly ahead on the screens. The star-chart identified it as Sol, a fourth magnitude star with nine planets. There was no other data; the system had never been surveyed.

Linx switched off the star-chart. He had hoped for something bigger. But he would head for the system. Within an inter-planetary atmosphere, spectronic flight was impossible. He might conceal for a little longer the extent to which the cruiser was damaged; he might even—if luck was with him—swing round the

13

blind side of one of those tiny planets and get in a cannonade at his pursuers.

It was worth trying. If he could destroy just one more Rutan ship, he would not be totally dishonoured in death.

Sol was looming on the screens, its central mass obscured by the blazing incandescence of its gases. Linx felt the cruiser slowing still further as it ploughed into the ion streams surrounding the star.

And a crazy idea occurred.

The dancing mantle of solar eruptions that concealed Sol's core would conceal the cruiser—if he could fly that close . . .

For a brief time—for perhaps twenty seconds—his starship's image would disappear from the screens of the pursuit ships. And if, during that time, he escaped in the scout ship . . . ?

Coldly, Linx calculated the risks. The little scout vessel, stored in the cruiser's underpod, was an inadequate ship. Its heat shields had not been devised to withstand solar temperatures. Its motors were comparatively puny, too—they might not pull the ship clear of Sol's gravity.

Then, finally, if he escaped from the sun and the Rutan fighters, hurtling on after his abandoned cruiser—finally he would still have to face the unguessable hazards of traversing the galaxy in a tiny craft intended only for shuttling between planets.

But such journeys had been made before. Linx remembered sagas about the heroes of antiquity. They would have considered the little scout a superbly equipped ship.

Already the blazing face of Sol was engulfing the screens. If he was going to make the attempt he would have to hurry. Swiftly, he programmed an orbital path above the star's surface. The cruiser's hull temperature was rising rapidly as he disconnected the recorders and carried them down to the scout ship.

There was no time for pre-flight checks. Settling behind the single console of the control bridge, Linx reached immediately for the emergency firing pin. He barely heard the muffled explosion of the launching rocket that catapulted the little scout ship out into space; the g-pressure was like a giant hand crushing him into unconsciousness . . .

Linx came round slowly. The rasping scream of the motors intruded first into his mind, warning that something was wrong even before he forced his eyes open. Acrid yellow smoke was curling through the vent tubes into the control bridge. He sat up and peered at the display panels. Seven minutes' elapsed flying time.

Even though it was apparent the little scout had suffered some grievous damage, Linx felt a surge of relief. That length of E.F.T. surely meant that his ruse had succeeded. The scout ship was clear of the sun and the Rutan fighters were already a million miles away in futile pursuit of the empty cruiser.

After all he had been through, the problem of nursing a sick craft across the galaxy to Sontara seemed comparatively easy. But as the deck computer analysed the damage the ship had sustained, Linx began to see the impossibility of his task. The scout's main drive had burned out. Its gravity plates had buckled in the heat of the sun and the pressure of the g-forces had sheared both gyro-stabilisers.

The computer went on to produce a list of smaller defects but Linx gave it little attention. Unless he could repair the ship he had no chance of ever seeing Sontara again. But to reach the main drive the ship would have to be completely stripped down. That meant making a landfall somewhere . . . if there proved to be a remotely suitable planet in this miserable little solar system.

With only nine planets in the system, Linx knew that the chances of one of them possessing a suitably breathable atmosphere were a million to one. He had little hope as he focused the spectograph on each in turn . . .

And the third planet, the little blue one, showed a reading of ninety four on the scale! Unbelievable luck! Linx gave a shout of delight and pointed the scout ship towards the planet. Now, he thought, if only the planet proved to be the home of some semi-intelligent species—and oxygen-rich planets often were—he could drum them into a labour force and be on his way back to Sontara within a matter of weeks.

Sontarans rarely smiled, except at the death throes of an enemy. But as his damaged ship flashed towards the third planet, Commander Jingo Linx allowed himself the smallest of satisfied smiles . . .

Irongron's Star

In the great hall of Irongron's castle they were holding a feast. The long banqueting table was lined with men-at-arms, chewing on stale bread and half-cooked meat, swigging rough red wine. It wasn't much of a feast, to be honest. But then, it wasn't much of a castle, either. And Captain Irongron and his men were as scruffy a bunch of cut-throats as you'd find in the length and breadth of Merrie England. Still, Irongron had ordered a carousal —and it wasn't healthy to argue.

Captain Irongron sat at the head of the long table chewing moodily on a leg of lamb. He was a great bull of a man, clad in steel and leather, a fierce black beard jutting from the massive chin. Beside him was Bloodaxe, his chief lieutenant, a long gangling fellow, with greasy yellow locks and a wispy beard grown in emulation of his beloved leader.

Irongron tore a chunk of bloody meat from the bone with his yellowing teeth, chewed, and glared and promptly spat it out. 'This sheep has been dead a year. Are they trying to poison me?'

Bloodaxe tried his own meat. It seemed no worse than usual. 'It was killed long since, Captain. But it's salted to preserve it.'

'Salted?' roared Irongron. 'It stinks!' He tossed the bone over his shoulder and it fell amongst the others that littered the rush-covered floor. 'Wine!' he bellowed. 'Must I die of thirst in my own hall? Bring me wine, I say!'

Meg, the serving wench, a burly woman who looked almost as tough as Irongron, scurried forward with a jug of wine and filled the pewter tankard clutched in Irongron's massive paw. Irongron swigged and spluttered . . . Meg ducked, just in time. The heavy tankard whizzed past her head and clanged against the stone wall. She backed away. ''Tis the dregs of the barrel, Captain, all there is left.'

Irongron glared mournfully round the hall. 'Sour wine! Stinking meat and sour wine! Is this how I am served?'

'Supplies are low, Captain,' said Bloodaxe placatingly. ''Tis some time since we went aforaging.'

Irongron nodded moodily. Not for the first time, he wondered if it had really been such a good idea to establish himself in his own castle. In the old days he and his band had roamed the forest like wolves, killing, plundering and moving on. They had had no shelter but the greenwood, but at least they had been free.

Then they had stumbled on the little castle, hidden deep in the forest. Its defences were crumbling, the moat dried-up, the drawbridge permanently down. There wasn't even a proper garrison. Its lord was away at the wars and he had left only a handful of retainers to defend his property.

Suddenly inspiration had come to Irongron. Why should he live the life of a hunted outlaw, when he could be as good as any nobleman, with a castle of his own? A night attack, the savage massacre of those within, and the castle had been his.

Now Irongron was a man of property—and his responsibilities weighed heavily upon him. True, he and his men were safe enough—for the moment. The castle although small was sturdy, and there was no force in the neighbourhood strong enough to winkle them out. Their nearest neighbour was one Sir Edward Fitzroy, but his castle was miles away. Moreover, Sir Edward was a sick man, wasted by fever brought home from the Crusades. The knight's son and most of his soldiers had been summoned by the king to his endless foreign wars, and his garrison was scarcely larger than Irongron's own.

It was the problem of supply that occupied Irongron's mind. He had a band of hungry fighting men who looked to him for constant supplies of food and wine and loot. For a time they had ridden out to plunder the countryside, returning to the castle at night. But after a few such raids the local peasants had grown wary, hiding their food and valuables. By now there just wasn't very much left to steal.

Irongron had considered leaving the castle and returning to the old roving life. But he had fallen into the trap of his new found status. He loved having his own great hall to feast in, being lord of his own castle. Why, he was almost respectable . . . There was one solution, he thought longingly. Sir Edward's castle would be a rich source of loot . . .

'We starve here, Bloodaxe,' he muttered. 'And meanwhile our good neighbour feasts his belly full with fresh meat, and swills down fine wine . . .'

'True enough, Captain. Sir Edward's cellars and store-houses are well stocked.'

Irongron grinned wolfishly. 'Perhaps we should relieve him of some of his abundance, eh, my friend? Surely he'd not begrudge us a little of his plenty . . .'

Bloodaxe wasn't listening. Instead he was staring out of the window, eyes wide in superstitious terror. 'Captain, look!'

Irongron looked. A fiery streak sped down through

the night sky. 'The stars!' yelled Bloodaxe. 'The stars are falling!'

Irongron shoved him aside. 'I see only one star—and it has fallen in the forest nearby.' He turned to his men-at-arms, eyes gleaming. 'Get up, you curs. Up, I say!'

Bloodaxe stared fearfully at him. 'Perhaps it is an omen—an evil sign.'

Irongron's men were as superstitious as they were savage and a frightened mutter of assent ran through the hall.

Irongron wasn't afraid. Somehow he felt sure the falling star was a good omen, a sign of his future greatness. 'That star is mine—Irongron's star. I shall have it. Fetch the horses—and hurry.'

Nobody moved.

'Hurry?' asked Bloodaxe slowly. 'Hurry where, Captain?'

'To find the star before some knave robs me of it. It landed close by . . .'

'But the forest is still in darkness. Who knows what demons might spring out upon us?'

Again the rumble of assent, louder this time. This was an age in which the powers of evil were very real, when old crones sold their souls to the devil for sinister powers, and sinners were frequently hauled off to hell with a clap of thunder and a stink of sulphur. The men of Irongron's band had plenty of sins on their consciences. None of them was anxious to meet the Evil One before time.

Irongron too was having second thoughts. He feared no mortal enemy—but witches and demons . . . The fears of his men allowed him to back down without loss of face. He sank back into his seat, muttering, 'Chicken-hearted knaves, every one of you.'

'It wants but a few hours till dawn, Captain,' said

Bloodaxe persuasively. 'Wait till then, till we can see what faces us. We'll follow you then.'

Irongron gave a surly nod. 'Let all be made ready. I ride at dawn—alone if need be.' He waved the rest of the band away, and they hurried out of the hall. Irongron slammed his fist down on the table. 'Bring me more wine!' Bloodaxe turned to retrieve the tankard from the floor, and Meg scurried forward with the jug. She filled two tankards to the brim, and Irongron raised his high. 'A toast,' he bellowed. 'A toast to Irongron's star!'

A few hours later a sorry-looking cavalcade clattered over the drawbridge into the forest. Quite a few toasts had followed the first, and Irongron and Bloodaxe were swaying in their saddles, red-eyed and very much the worse for wear. Behind them rode half-a-dozen men-at-arms, all that Bloodaxe had been able to kick into wakefulness. It was the dawn of a fine summer morning. Shafts of sunlight slanted down across the forest paths, the birds were singing and the dew sparkled on the grass, but Irongron and his followers were in no state to appreciate the beauties of nature.

Soon Irongron reined in his horse and pointed. 'Look!' A column of black smoke was rising above the trees. 'There, lads. There it is.' His bloodshot eyes blazed with excitement.

Bloodaxe was less enthusiastic. 'Careful, Captain. This looks like devil's work to me.'

Irongron ignored him. 'A star—a fallen star. Perhaps it is made of gold.'

The horses were prancing and bucking restlessly, as if they sensed something strange in the forest ahead. 'What ails the beasts?' growled Irongron. 'Down, lads, we'll go forward on foot.' They dismounted, tethered the horses, and moved cautiously through the forest, Irongron and Bloodaxe in the lead, the rest trailing as far behind as they dared.

The column of smoke was coming from a clearing in the forest. Not a natural clearing but one newly-made, a huge black circle scorched out of the forest green. Around its edges fire still flickered here and there and in its centre was a metal globe, half-buried in the smoke-blackened earth. The metal plates of its hull were twisted with heat.

Irongron drew his sword, and Bloodaxe took a firmer grip on his battleaxe. 'A star,' breathed Irongron again. 'A fallen star . . .'

There was a whine of power and a door opened in the side of the metal sphere. An extraordinary figure stepped out. It wore silvery armour, with a massive metal collar about the neck. A huge domed helmet covered the head. The strange being was short, but broad, and gave an impression of tremendous, compact power.

Bloodaxe and the others fell back, but Irongron stood his ground. 'A warrior,' he growled. 'Do you come to challenge me, sky warrior?' Confident in his size and strength, Irongron strode forward, raising his great sword in a two-handed grip. He was about to split the strange mannikin down the middle—when the creature whipped a gleaming metal device from its belt. The device glowed briefly and there was a sudden high-pitched buzz and the sword flew from Irongron's hand.

Irongron's men broke and ran. Only the faithful Bloodaxe hovered on the edge of the clearing. 'Fly, Captain,' he called. 'Fly for your life.'

Irongron stood amazed, rubbing a sword-arm gone suddenly numb. 'What creature is this?'

22

Bloodaxe had no doubts. 'It is a devil from hell. Run, Captain!'

The creature returned the device to its belt, and a gauntleted hand touched some kind of control. There was a crackle of static, then a booming metallic voice, speaking strangely accented but clearly understandable English. 'Peace,' it said. 'Fear not. I shall not harm you.'

Irongron was too astonished to be afraid. 'It speaks,' he whispered. 'Who are you, star warrior? Where do you come from?'

'I am a Sontaran officer. My name is Linx.'

Satisfied the creature was not immediately dangerous, Bloodaxe edged nearer. 'Did he say he is a Saracen, Captain? I have heard tales of their eastern magic.'

The creature was going about some strange ritual of its own. It thrust the metal rod into the ground and stepped back. To the astonishment of the watchers, a metallic flag bearing some alien device sprang from the rod, and flapped in the morning breeze. At the same time, a weird melody floated from the open door of the little sphere.

The creature raised one arm in a stiff salute. The metallic voice boomed out again. 'By virtue of my authority as an officer of the Sontaran Army Space Corps, I hereby claim this planet, its moons and satellites, for the greater glory of the Sontaran empire.'

Irongron, Bloodaxe and the others looked on in some puzzlement. They didn't know it, but the Earth had just been taken over.

2

Linx's Bargain

Some time later, Irongron and Linx were confronting each other in the great hall. They were surrounded by a semi-circle of Irongron's men, clutching an assortment of spears, bows, swords and axes. Irongron had decided to take Linx captive. Fortunately, the alien had seemed willing enough to accompany them back to the castle.

Irongron stared grimly at his prisoner, wondering what he was going to do with him. 'Why have you come here, star warrior? What do you want of us?'

'Your help.'

'Help you? Why should I help you? Why should I not slay you and take your ship and its treasures for myself?'

'The ship is useless to you—it is in need of repair. Even if it were not, you would destroy yourself should you tamper with it.'

'Then why should I not slay you for sport? Can you overcome all of us with your magic?'

The Sontaran stiffened with anger at the threat. Then he forced himself to be calm. If these primitives nerved themselves to attack, there were enough of them to hack him to pieces. He must bargain for survival. He looked at the fierce figures surrounding him. Warriors of a kind certainly, every one was carrying some kind of cutting weapon. But no explosive devices or they would surely have produced them. A warlike but still primitive culture, decided Linx—and knew what he must do. He addressed the leader. 'You are a soldier, are you not? A warrior?'

Irongron's enormous chest swelled with pride. 'I took this castle by force of arms. Those who held it, I slew. All the countryside around here pays me tribute.'

'Yet no doubt you have enemies? Other warriors who envy your good fortune?'

'Aye, many. But they cannot harm me. Their troops are all at the wars.'

'And when they return?'

Irongron shrugged. 'Then we must fight.'

'I can give you weapons to fight with. Weapons that will make you master, so none dare stand against you. You shall take what—castles you will.'

'Magic weapons?' asked Irongron eagerly. 'Like that which smote my sword from my hand?'

Linx had no intention of providing his captors with weapons equal to his own. The simplest of percussion weapons would be more than good enough for them. 'Other weapons, fitter for your purpose,' he said enticingly. 'Weapons to strike a man dead from far away. Magic fires that can tumble castle walls. You can be supreme warrior!'

'I can be king,' said Irongron slowly. 'And what do you ask in return—other than your life?'

'Shelter. A place to conceal myself and my ship from prying eyes, and help with its repair. You have men who can work in metal?'

'An armourer to sharpen weapons. A blacksmith with a forge. If this will serve your needs . . .'

Linx could make the promised weapons with such simple resources, but his own needs were far more complex. 'I need more, much more . . . There is damage to the drive mechanism of my ship. I need special alloys, skilled technicians, complex electronic circuitry.'

Irongron stared blankly at him. 'We have none of these things.'

Linx considered. He had landed on a primitive planet in a pre-technical era. Yet there were advantages. No one in this age would have the instruments to track him down, or the weapons to oppose him. On the other hand, to repair his ship he needed skills and materials this age had not yet developed. Since the ship was damaged, he could scarcely move in space. He would have to use the osmic projector, part of the scout ship's emergency kit. With its temporal transporter beam, he could go forward in time and—

Irongron's voice interrupted his thoughts . . .

'Do you hear me, star warrior? I said we have none of the things of which you speak.'

The great domed head swung slowly towards him. 'Then I must take them from those who have,' said Commander Linx.

An army staff-car drew up at the gates of the big country house. One of the passengers in the back seat wore the uniform of a full Brigadier, beside him was a tall man with a lined young-old face and a shock of white hair. This second passenger was strangely and colourfully dressed in narrow trousers, a frilled white shirt, a velvet jacket and a flowing cloak.

There was a gleaming new barbed-wire fence around the house, and an armed sentry at the gate. The sergeant-driver produced passes which were scrutinised with minute care. Finally, the sentry waved the car on. Another soldier opened the massive iron gates, and the car drove through, pulling up before the flight of steps that led into the house. The Brigadier and his companion got out and went inside.

The Brigadier led the way through an imposing

26

entrance-hall where white-coated scientists bustled to and fro, and cursing soldiers manhandled heavy crates of equipment. They went up a broad, curving staircase, along a corridor, and into a very long first-floor room, which ran across the front of the house. It had once been the main drawing-room, but was now being converted into a kind of dormitory. Soldiers were busily erecting partitioned cubicles. Nails were being hammered home, hinges screwed into place, and still more soldiers staggered in with camp beds and piles of blankets.

The tall man looked round the noisy chaotic scene without enthusiasm. '*Here*, Brigadier?'

'I'm afraid so, Doctor. Not exactly the Ritz, I know. But it's no joke providing emergency accommodation for so many people.'

The Doctor sighed. 'All right, you've had your little bit of mystification. Now you've shown me where I'm supposed to stay, perhaps you wouldn't mind telling me why?'

The Brigadier looked at him thoughtfully. He'd been worried about his old friend for quite some time. Ever since his assistant Jo Grant had surprised everyone suddenly, by getting married, the Doctor had been unusually irritable. He had brusquely refused the offer of a new assistant, saying he'd manage on his own. The Brigadier knew that the Doctor missed Jo, and he also knew that the Doctor was far too stubborn to admit it. When a new and puzzling problem had come up, the Brigadier had almost welcomed it. What the Doctor needed was a really good scientific mystery . . .

'Well, Brigadier?' asked the Doctor sharply. 'Are you going to tell me or aren't you?'

Hurriedly the Brigadier assembled his thoughts. 'Yes, of course. Well, now, this place is one of the most top-secret research establishments in the country. Most of their work's so secret they don't even know what they're doing themselves.'

The Doctor ignored the Brigadier's little joke. 'And?'

'It's also one of the best-guarded places in the country. Security details, alarm systems, the lot.'

'I gathered that when we arrived. For a time I thought they weren't going to let *you* in.'

The Brigadier coughed. 'Quite so. Place is almost too security-conscious. Makes it all the more puzzling.'

'Makes *what* all the more puzzling? Come on, Brigadier, how can I help you unless you tell me what's going on?'

'Things vanishing,' said the Brigadier mysteriously.

'What sort of things?'

'So far they've lost nearly a dozen leading scientists and several million pounds' worth of top-secret electronic equipment.'

'What sort of research goes on here?'

'Space hardware mostly. New alloys, guidance systems, methods of propulsion . . .'

The Doctor rubbed his chin. 'I see . . . All right. What action have you taken so far?'

'I had a bright idea,' said the Brigadier modestly. 'You see, the scientists and their labs were scattered all over the area. Pretty hard to keep an eye on. I've centralised everything in this one place, confined the whole lot of 'em to barracks. Until we find out what's going on, they'll all live on the job. All the eggs in one basket, so to speak.'

'As long as no one steals the basket,' said the Doctor sardonically. 'Does it occur to you, Brigadier, that by putting all your scientists and their equipment in one building you may actually be making things easier for your mysterious enemy?'

'Maybe so, Doctor. But if he attacks, he's got to

attack *here*. And you'll be waiting for him. I've fixed up a cover story, you'll be assigned to one of the research teams.'

The Doctor stood gazing into space, and the Brigadier held his breath. Suddenly the Doctor smiled. 'All right, Brigadier, I'll be your guinea pig. I'll need full details of the missing scientists. What their specialities were, when and where they disappeared . . . And a list of the missing equipment. I shall need some equipment of my own too—including the TARDIS.'

The Brigadier gave him a suspicious look. Since the Time Lords had now lifted their sentence of exile, the Doctor remained on Earth by choice rather than necessity. But he disappeared in the TARDIS more and more frequently these days, and the Brigadier couldn't help fearing that one day his old friend would vanish for ever. 'What do you need the TARDIS for?'

'Because if your troubles are due to some kind of alien interference, I'll need the TARDIS to track it to its source. By now your missing scientists may be a very long way away . . .'

The huge storage cellar beneath Irongron's castle had undergone some extraordinary changes. The far end of the long room was filled by the gleaming sphere that was Linx's scout ship. Dragged from the forest by teams of sweating horses, it had been hauled into the castle and down into the cellars, on an extraordinary arrangement of rollers and pulleys devised by Linx. Irongron had driven his men mercilessly until at last the scout ship was installed to Linx's satisfaction.

The rest of the cellar had been transformed into a kind of workshop. Wooden tables along the stone walls were packed with an amazing jumble of equipment— the dis-assembled damaged engines of the ship and the tools and equipment Linx needed to repair it. The ship's computer had been installed against one wall. Cables ran from the ship to the computer, and to the power tools being used by the men working at the different tables. They were a strange, motley-looking group of men, dressed in a variety of twentieth-century clothing. Some wore white laboratory coats, others were in their pyjamas. All were dirty, ragged, thin, clearly on the point of exhaustion. Nevertheless, all worked with obsessive concentration.

Linx stood at the computer console. He adjusted a control, and the scientists increased the pace of their work. Linx nodded in satisfaction. The minds of the men he had kidnapped from the twentieth-century were linked to the computer by relay beam. They had become, in fact, little more than extensions of Linx himself, their hands and brains totally devoted to his purpose.

There was still much to be done. Although the main generators were still working, the drive unit of his ship had been badly damaged. Parts could be repaired, other parts would have to be completely remade, forged afresh from unsatisfactory materials by relatively unskilled hands. It would be a long and difficult task, but Linx had no doubt that he would succeed—eventually.

Unfortunately the human slaves lacked stamina. Their feeble bodies tended to collapse under the unceasing toil. He needed more slaves, he decided, and more equipment too. It was time to plan another raid on the future.

There came a tremendous banging on the cellar door.

3

Sarah's Bluff

Linx's slave-workers ignored the insistent noise—they didn't even hear it. Their minds were totally closed to anything but the never-ending tasks imposed upon them.

Linx went to the cellar door. It was closed and locked but he made no attempt to open it. 'Linx!' bellowed a hoarse voice from the other side. 'My lord Linx, will you open the door?'

'None may enter here,' said the Sontaran. 'Such was my agreement with your Captain.'

From the other side of the door Bloodaxe shouted, 'It is my Captain who sends me. He would have you help him test the new weapon you have given him.'

'Tell him I am occupied. Now, leave me to my work.'

There came a final thump on the door and Bloodaxe moved away.

'Insolent primitives,' muttered Linx. 'Did I not need their aid . . .'

He glanced across at a side table where a couple of scientists were assembling the lock mechanism of a crude percussion rifle. They were the only ones engaged in such work, and it would have been immediately clear to any observer that most of Linx's resources were being reserved for the repair of his space ship, and only a small proportion given to making the promised weapons for Irongron. Linx had good reason for keeping Irongron and his men away.

Bloodaxe found his Captain wedging an apple into one

of the torch brackets. Satisfied, Irongron stepped back. 'Well? Where is our star warrior?'

'He will not come, Captain. He says he is busy.'

'Insolent barbarian,' growled Irongron. 'Did I not need his aid . . . Still, no matter. See, Bloodaxe, the first of our new weapons.' He pointed to the clumsy-looking rifle on the table. In appearance it was rather like an early musket (still not invented on Earth) though it was breech-loading rather than muzzle loading. It fired a heavy bullet, enclosed in a massive cartridge, and it was powerful enough to punch through armour at close range. A leather bag of cartridges lay beside it.

In Irongron's age, weapons like this were still unknown. In time to come they would end the supremacy of the man in armour, and the great cannon would bring down the walls of the proudest castle. Irongron was a fighting man by instinct, and he could see the potential of the weapon in his hands. A small force armed with weapons like these could put an army to flight.

Irongron picked up the rifle and went to the far end of the hall. He raised the clumsy weapon and fired. There was a thunderous explosion and a cloud of black smoke. A chip of stone flew from the wall—about a foot away from the torch-holder.

Bloodaxe jumped back in alarm. 'By heavens, Captain, it claps the ears.'

'I shall master the aim soon enough,' said Irongron impatiently. He ejected the used cartridge, went to the table for another. Bloodaxe looked on fearfully. 'Is it magic, Captain?'

Irongron inserted a fresh cartridge. 'It is a mighty weapon, Bloodaxe. Sharper than a spear, faster than an arrow. Linx has served me well.'

Bloodaxe crossed himself. 'Do not trust him, Captain. We meddle with the powers of darkness. They may yet bring death and destruction to us all.'

Irongron was back at his firing position. 'The death and destruction will be for our enemies.' There was another deafening explosion and this time the apple leaped from its place on the wall. Irongron picked it up. There was a round hole clear through the centre. 'See, I have cut out the core!'

The Doctor looked on as half-a-dozen sweating soldiers wrestled the TARDIS into position just outside his cubicle door. 'All right, that'll do.' The corporal in charge of the squad saluted and led his men away.

The Doctor was about to go in when a spry white-haired old fellow in a white coat wandered up to him. He peered at the TARDIS through enormously thick spectacles, and said briskly, 'Rubeish.'

'I beg your pardon?'

'Rubeish. Professor Joseph Rubeish.' He held out his hand.

'Oh, I see. How do you do?'

They shook hands and the old man said. 'Disgraceful, of course. Utterly disgraceful.'

'What is?'

'Shutting us up here like this. Like a lot of kids kept in after school. It's all that Brigadier's fault. Military idiot!'

The Doctor smiled. 'I sometimes feel the same way myself. Still, he means well, you know.'

'Haven't seen my wife and family for three days,' said Rubeish confidentially.

'I'm sorry . . .'

The old man gave a malicious grin. 'Just shows, there's always a silver lining! And your name?'

The Doctor produced his usual alias. 'Smith. Doctor John Smith.'

33

Rubeish sniffed. 'Seem to be a lot of 'em about today.'

'I'm sorry?'

Rubeish nodded to a cubicle on the other side of the room. Through the open door they could see an attractive dark-haired girl unpacking a small suitcase. 'That young lady over there is also called Smith.' He waved to the girl, who looked up and smiled back. Rather a nice smile, thought the Doctor.

Rubeish called, 'Miss Smith! Come and meet your namesake.' The girl came over to them, and the old man performed the introductions with an old-world flourish. 'Miss Lavinia Smith, Doctor John Smith.' The Doctor and the girl shook hands. Rubeish went off on another of his sudden tangents. 'Doctor, I am intrigued. What's that thing for?' He pointed to the TARDIS.

The Doctor sighed. Rubeish seemed a pleasant enough old boy but it was clear that he was as curious as he was garrulous—and the Doctor had work to do. 'It contains my equipment, Professor.'

'How original.' Rubeish went over to the TARDIS and began studying it, his nose a few inches from the side.

The Doctor looked thoughtfully down at the girl. 'You'll be the well-known virologist, Miss Smith?'

She gave him a nervous smile. 'That's right. Who told you?'

'I recently read your paper on the teleological response of the virus. A most impressive piece of work.'

'Thank you.' The girl seemed anxious to get away.

Smoothly the Doctor went on. 'Particularly since it came out about twenty years ago. You must have written it when you were about five years old.'

'Ah . . . yes, that is rather difficult to explain, isn't it?'

'I'm sure you'll try.'

The girl took a deep breath. 'Lavinia Smith is my

aunt. She's in America on a lecture tour. She got an invitation to come here and I took her place.'

'Why?'

'There have been all kinds of rumours about mysterious goings-on here. I thought I might get an inside story. I'm a free-lance journalist—my name's Sarah Jane Smith.'

The Doctor frowned down at her. 'You realise this is a rather dangerous place to be at the moment?'

'I can't help that, I'm here now. Anyway there are all those soldiers to look after us. Are you going to give me away, Doctor?'

'No, I don't think so.'

'Why not? I might be a spy.'

'A real spy would have come up with a more convincing story. Anyway you can make yourself useful. We need someone around to make the tea.'

The Doctor couldn't have made a more unfortunate joke. Sarah had been making her own way in a man's world for some years now, and she strongly resented any suggestion that her sex doomed her to an inferior role. 'If you think I'm going to spend my time here dancing attendance on you . . .' she flared.

The Doctor wasn't listening. He had just noticed that Rubeish had abandoned his study of the TARDIS, taken a bit of chalk from his pocket, and was busily chalking a long and complicated equation on the side of the police box. The Doctor hurried over. 'My dear Professor, kindly desist at once! This is neither a blackboard nor a public convenience.'

Rubeish blinked up at him. 'I do beg your pardon. This equation has been worrying me, you see, and I was just trying to prove . . . Oh dear, oh dear, what *was* I trying to prove?'

The Doctor produced his key and unlocked the

TARDIS door. Sarah looked at him in surprise. 'What are you going to do in there?'

'Make myself a cup of tea,' said the Doctor with dignity. He opened the TARDIS door and went inside, closing it behind him.

Sarah walked round the police box, shaking her head. She came back to Rubeish. 'Do you know that man?'

'You've a short memory, young lady. I've just introduced you.'

'No, I mean how long have you known him?'

Rubeish produced a large old-fashioned watch. 'A little over two minutes. Why?'

'I think there's something rather odd about him.'

'Well, he's a new arrival with an unlikely name.' Rubeish gave one of his malicious smiles. 'But then, so are you, young lady . . .'

'Well, yes,' said Sarah hurriedly. 'But all the same . . .'

Abruptly Rubeish said, 'Mind you, I think I agree with you. Any scientist who keeps his equipment in an old police box . . .' His voice tailed off, and he gazed abstractedly into space. Suddenly he began chalking a fresh equation on the side of the police box. There came an indignant knocking from inside. Rubeish shook his head sadly and wandered away.

Sarah went back to her own tiny cubicle and resumed her unpacking. There *was* something strange about the Doctor, she was sure of it. For one thing, he'd accepted her story far too readily. Perhaps he had good reasons to avoid contact with the authorities. Perhaps he was a spy himself—the enemy might well have planted an inside man. Sarah decided not to go to bed after all. Instead she would stay awake—and keep an eye on the Doctor.

4

Irongron's Captive

The castle of Sir Edward Fitzroy lay on the other side of
the forest. It was a handsome, well-cared-for building,
very different from Irongron's scruffy little stronghold.
The grey stone battlements of the castle towered high
above the tree tops. Three of the castle's four walls
were protected by a broad semi-circular moat while the
fourth backed on to the forest.

But for all its impressive appearance, Sir Edward's
castle was no more than a hollow shell. A castle of this
size needed a large garrison to defend it—and Sir
Edward had only a few old men and boys at his command.

Tall and frail, still wasted by the fever he had
brought back from the Holy Land, Sir Edward sat in his
private chamber, patiently waiting for his wife to run
out of words.

It was a considerable wait. The Lady Eleanor was a
woman of spirit, and she had never lacked the ability to
express her feelings. Her subject this morning, as on
many others, was the robber Irongron. 'How long,
Edward?' she demanded. 'How long will you tolerate
this upstart, this robbing usurper as our neighbour?
He robs, he pillages, he murders . . . He flouts your
authority every day—the authority which comes from
the King!'

Sir Edward sighed. 'Unfortunately the King who
gave me my authority has deprived me of the troops I
need to maintain it.'

'Irongron's band is small. We still have Hal the archer, and a few men-at-arms.'

'Too few to stand against Irongron and his cut-throats. But never fear, my lady, I shall act against Irongron. I have done so this very day.'

'How so, my lord?'

Sir Edward rose painfully and went to the window, staring out over the endless vista of waving treetops. 'I have sent Eric, my squire, with a letter to old Lord Salisbury. Like myself Salisbury has but a handful of men. Yet if our men are combined, they may yet make a force that will crush this Irongron.'

Lady Eleanor doubted that they would do any such thing. Moreover Lord Salisbury had troubles of his own, and was unlikely to concern himself with the problems of his neighbour. She looked at Sir Edward's hopeful face, and decided to keep her doubts to herself. 'You will excuse me, my lord? I have much to do.'

As she made her way down to the castle kitchen, Lady Eleanor's mind was filled with concern for her husband. He was a simple man, brave and honourable, but he had sacrificed his health in the service of his King. Now, in his weakened state, he lacked the ruthlessness needed to deal with such rogues as Irongron.

Hal the archer leaned broad shoulders against the kitchen wall and watched Mary, the youngest and prettiest of the serving wenches, as she stirred the cauldron of soup that hung over the fire. 'Never fear, my girl,' he boasted. 'You have the finest archer in England to protect you. Else Irongron's men would snap up so tasty a morsel in no time.'

Mary giggled. 'Oh indeed? And if you're so fine a warrior, why aren't you at the wars with the others?'

Hal yawned and stretched. 'I've had my fill of war,

38

my sweet. I followed Sir Edward to the Crusades—aye, and brought him back again when his fever laid him low.'

Mary looked sideways at him. 'Oh—'tis not that you're too timid then?'

'Timid?' roared Hal. He nodded to the longbow that leaned against the wall not far from his hand. 'Why, if you were a man I'd put a quiverful of arrows through you. Since you're a wench I'll take a kiss instead.'

He reached for Mary, who dodged him and ran away laughing. Hal caught her and kissed her soundly—just as Lady Eleanor appeared in the doorway.

Hal and Mary sprang apart and the girl said hurriedly, 'It was all the fault of this archer fellow, my lady.'

Eleanor said calmly, 'Fetch a flagon of our finest wine and take it to Sir Edward. He is in low spirits, and it may cheer him.'

'Yes my lady, at once my lady.' Mary scurried from the room.

Hal picked up his bow. 'I must go and check the guard. Old men doze easily. Be not too harsh with her, my lady. The fault was mine.'

'That I can believe.' Lady Eleanor looked thoughtfully at him. He was a tall young fellow with yellow Saxon hair and a brown, cheerful face. 'The finest archer in England, you say?'

Hal reddened, but said stoutly, 'I know none better.'

'Would you do your lord a great service—even at the risk of your life?'

'Of course, my lady.'

Lady Eleanor came closer. 'Then mark me well. I have a fitting target for your arrows.'

His heart full of the importance of his mission, Squire

Eric rode swiftly through the forest. He was mounted on the finest horse in the Castle stables, and a new sword hung at his side. This was the most dangerous part of his journey, the point where the road came closest to Irongron's castle. He touched his breast, reassured by the crackle of the message-parchment thrust inside his tunic. If Irongron's men ambushed him, they would never take him alive, he vowed. And before they killed him, he would destroy the vital message. Still, better to take no chances. He touched spurs to his horse's flanks, and the animal broke into a gallop. Eric thundered along the forest trail, his mind filled with glorious visions. He saw himself encountering Irongron on the road, defeating him in single combat, returning home in triumph. He rounded the bend in the road at a gallop. An invisible force swept him out of his saddle and slammed him to the ground.

The impact knocked him senseless. When he recovered he saw a circle of ragged grim-faced men standing over him. Their leader, a tall, lank-haired, bony fellow, clasped a mighty war-axe. Nearby, one of the band was untying a rope from the trunk of a tree. Bitterly Eric realised he had fallen victim to the simplest of traps, a thin rope stretched across the road.

He took the message from inside his tunic and made a hopeless attempt to cram it into his mouth. The parchment was snatched away, he was hauled to his feet, bound, and thrown across the saddle of his horse. Soon the little group rode away, one of them leading the captive's horse. Dazedly, Eric realised he was being taken captive to Irongron's castle. He knew what awaited him there—torture and death. He clenched his jaws, and prayed for the courage to die without speaking.

Bloodaxe dragged his prisoner into the great hall and

thrust him before Irongron's chair. 'We caught this little rabbit in the forest, Captain.'

Irongron looked thoughtfully at the prisoner, who did his best to stare boldly back. Despite his bedraggled appearance the lad was richly dressed. 'A person of some importance,' growled Irongron thoughtfully. 'Sir Edward's squire, perhaps?'

Eric said nothing. Irongron drew the knife from his belt, and held it to his throat. 'Are you loyal to your lord, boy?'

'I am,' said Eric steadily.

'We shall see . . .' promised Irongron menacingly.

Bloodaxe produced a roll of parchment. 'He was carrying this. He tried to eat it when we caught him.'

Irongron laughed. 'Are Sir Edward's men so ill fed?' He unrolled the parchment and peered at it. 'Bah, I can make nothing of their Norman scribbles. What does it say?'

He gave it back to Bloodaxe, who stared blankly at it. 'I know not, Captain. I cannot read.' Nor could anyone else in the castle.

Irongron loomed menacingly over Eric. 'Well, boy? What does the message say? Does your Sir Edward plan to attack me? Speak!'

'I shall tell you nothing.'

Irongron grinned wolfishly at Bloodaxe. 'Take him below. We shall find means to loosen his tongue—after supper.'

Sir Edward sat huddled over the fire, staring abstractedly into the flickering flames. He looked up eagerly as Lady Eleanor came into the room. 'Is Eric back?'

Eleanor shook her head. She looked at a side table where bread, meat and fruit stood untouched. 'You've not eaten all day.'

Sir Edward went to the window and stared out. Darkness was gathering over the forest. 'Why has Eric not returned? He has had time to ride to Salisbury's castle three times over.'

'It is not good for you to worry so much.'

'How can I not worry?'

Lady Eleanor came to stand at his side. 'Think that tomorrow will be brighter, my lord.' Sir Edward stared at her in surprise, sensing some hidden meaning in her words. She smiled enigmatically.

'Edward, I have heard that Irongron walks his battlements each morning at sunrise.'

Sir Edward nodded gloomily. 'He struts the wall like a cockerel, they say. No doubt it pleases him to be so high.'

'Does he climb so high that one of Hal's arrows could not reach him?'

'You speak in riddles, my lady.'

'I have sent Hal to hide in the woods by Irongron's castle. When tomorrow's sun rises, Irongron will walk his battlements for the last time.'

Sir Edward was shocked. 'But that is not honourable, my lady. It is murder.'

'It is execution,' said Eleanor resolutely. 'And a villain such as Irongron deserves no better.'

Irongron was practising sword-play in the great hall, wielding the great battle-sword that few other men could even lift. Torch-light glinted on the steel as he swung the mighty weapon like a toy, finishing with a flurry of slashing blows that would have reduced any opponent to mincemeat. Breathing hard, Irongron sheathed his sword, and drained the flagon of wine that stood on the table. Suddenly he sensed he was being watched and swung round, hand flying to his sword-hilt. A squat powerful figure in silvery armour stood in the doorway.

'Linx!' roared Irongron delightedly. 'So, you obey my summons at last, do you? By the stars, you cut a fine figure in that armour of yours.'

The alien voice boomed from beneath the helmet. 'It is a Sontaran space suit, Lord Irongron.'

'But why must we never see your face, good Linx?'

'This helmet conceals the fact that I am not of your kind.' A dry rasping chuckle came from beneath the helmet. 'You might find my true appearance—unpleasing.'

Irongron laughed. 'By my sword, Linx, I'll wager you are the fairest beauty in my castle.'

Linx had no use for social chit-chat. 'Why do you continually summon me? My work is pressing. I have much to do this night.'

Irongron tugged his beard. He had no very good reason for summoning his strange guest, merely a burning curiosity about what was happening in Linx's workshop. Suddenly an excuse popped into his head. 'I have a prisoner in my dungeons, Lord Linx, a surly fellow. Despite all the persuasions of my men, he will not speak.'

'You wish him to give you information? Then give him to me. I will make him speak.'

Irongron glanced at the guard by the doorway, saw that the man was dozing, and hurled an empty tankard with savage accuracy. The guard jerked awake as the tankard rebounded from his helmet with a clang. 'Tell Bloodaxe to fetch up the prisoner.' Irongron poured himself more wine, chuckling delightedly. 'Ah, Linx, you cunning devil, what fresh tricks of torture can you show me, eh?'

'What is the nature of the information that you seek?'

43

Irongron stared blankly at him. 'How should I know? Plots, conspiracies—our prisoner is a messenger of one who seeks to make war against me.'

'War? That is excellent.'

'Oh,' said Irongron. 'So you like war, eh?'

There was a note of fierce eagerness in the Sontaran's voice. 'Who does not? My race has been at war for centuries. One day our space fleets will subjugate every galaxy in the universe!' Irongron stared blankly at him, and the Sontaran turned away in disgust. 'You do not understand me. I am stranded here on this filthy primitive planet when I should be leading my squadron to glory. I am an expert at war, Irongron!'

Astonished at the sudden passion in Linx's voice, Irongron said uneasily, 'That's as maybe. Meanwhile, what about the weapons you promised?'

'Some you have already. There will be more. Keep your side of the bargain, and I shall keep mine.'

Irongron scowled blackly for a moment then gave a great rumbling laugh. 'We make good allies, Linx. Each has much that the other needs.'

Linx said nothing. A moment later a little group of men entered the hall. Bloodaxe was in the lead and behind him came men-at-arms dragging Eric, Sir Edward's squire. His face was bruised and bloody, and it was clear that he had been badly beaten, but his jaws were still clamped shut, and there was a gleam of defiance in his eyes.

'Has he spoken yet?' growled Irongron.

'He has a stout heart, this one, Captain. He has said not a word.' There was a note almost of admiration in Bloodaxe's voice.

'Good!' Irongron turned to the Sontaran. 'A fair measure for you, Linx.'

'Very well. Hold him still.'

Eric looked at the Sontaran in horror. Irongron's men were bad enough, but at least they were human enemies. Somehow he knew that this squat armoured figure was something strange, evil, totally alien.

He struggled wildly in the grip of his captors as Linx advanced steadily towards him.

5

The Doctor Disappears

Linx marched up to the struggling squire and stood looking into his face. Then he reached into the pouch at his belt and produced a slim metal rod. He adjusted a control and held the rod up to the prisoner's face. A light glowed briefly on its end, and there was a faint electronic hum.

Eric stopped struggling. He straightened up, his eyes wide and staring, and stood passively waiting. Linx turned away.

'Well, come on, Linx,' bellowed Irongron. 'Have at him!'

'I have finished. Ask him what you wish.'

'But you have done nothing!'

Linx held up the metal tube. 'This is a key. I have unlocked your prisoner's mind. Question him.'

Irongron walked slowly up to Eric and stared into his blank face. 'How many men guard Sir Edward's castle?'

'There are but ten in the garrison now,' said Eric promptly. 'Old men for the most part, save Hal the archer.'

Bloodaxe looked at Irongron in astonishment, and took a pace back, crossing himself. ''Tis witchcraft!'

Irongron went on with his questioning. 'And does he plan to attack me with his ten old men?'

'He sent me with a message to Lord Salisbury, asking for aid. If he succeeds in raising a force against you, then he will attack.'

'Listen to the fellow, Bloodaxe. He cannot babble fast enough!' Suddenly he noticed Linx moving towards the door. 'Stay, Linx. Have I given you leave to go?'

The Sontaran ignored him. In a spurt of rage, Irongron snatched up an axe and sprang in front of Linx, raising the weapon menacingly.

The metal tube was still in Linx's hand. He raised it, the end glowed again, brighter this time, and a beam of light sheared through the axe-haft just below the head. The axe-blade fell on to the flagstone with a clang, and suddenly Irongron was clutching a useless wooden pole.

Linx thrust past him. 'Each of us has much to do, Lord Irongron, and we are wasting time. I will be back.'

Irongron flung down the axe-haft in a rage. 'The insolent dog! By my sword, Bloodaxe, I shall pickle that star warrior of ours in boiling oil before I have done with him.' He swung round on the prisoner, who still stood gazing blankly ahead. 'Now, lad, tell me of the defences of Sir Edward's castle.'

Everything was quiet in the Research Centre. Most of the scientists had retired to their cubicles for the night. The Doctor however was still very much awake. He sat on the end of his bed, assembling a complicated looking apparatus from an assortment of electronic parts, which he was taking from a small black box. Someone appeared in the cubicle doorway. It was Professor Rubeish, glasses pushed up on his forehead, spiky white hair on end with excitement. 'Miss Smith!' he exclaimed dramatically.

'Wrong cubicle, Professor. I'm the Doctor. Why don't you try keeping your glasses on the end of your nose?'

The old man pulled the glasses back into place, and peered at the Doctor through thick pebble lenses.

'Listen, Doctor. Miss Smith is not Miss Smith!'

'She isn't?'

'No. And in that case—who is she?'

The Doctor put down his sonic screwdriver and sighed. 'I'm not sure I understand you, Professor.'

'I just bumped into Sir Matthew Dingle, the bio-physicist. I told him I was on the same landing as Lavinia Smith the virologist, and do you know what he said?'

'He said she's in her late sixties, and in addition she's in America.'

'He said she's . . .' began Rubeish, then broke off, staring indignantly at the Doctor. 'How did you know that?' He took a step towards the Doctor and bumped into the bedside table and nearly sent the Doctor's apparatus flying. The Doctor grabbed it just in time.

'Do be careful, my dear Rubeish. This is rather delicate equipment.'

'Suppose she's a spy? What would we do?'

'Shoot her?' suggested the Doctor cheerfully. 'Oh, come on, Rubeish, she can't do any harm. She's just a slip of a girl.'

'It's the mind that can be dangerous, Doctor,' said Rubeish solemnly. 'Some women can think almost as well as a man. Do you know, she tried to tell me *you* were a spy. Typical female cunning that.'

At this rather unfortunate moment Sarah popped her head into the cubicle. 'Ah there you are. I wasn't sure if I was on the right floor.'

The excuse was feeble enough, and Rubeish glared suspiciously at her. 'Goodnight,' he snapped and scurried into his own cubicle, slamming the door behind him.

Sarah looked at the apparatus on the Doctor's table. It seemed to contain valves, condensers, and a number

48

of oddly-shaped aerials. 'What is that thing, Doctor?'

'My alarm clock.'

'Oh, don't be so patronising. What is it really?'

The Doctor straightened up. 'This, my dear young lady, is a rhondium sensor. It detects the presence of delta particles. At a pre-fixed spectrum density an oscillation begins in this cylinder here, which opens a vacuum valve, which triggers an alarm bell, which wakes me up. Clear?'

'Why do you want to be woken up when it detects delta particles?,

'I happen to be very interested in delta particles,' snapped the Doctor. 'Why do you ask so many questions?'

'Because I'm a journalist.' Sarah noticed that the Doctor was stretching out in the armchair beside his bed. 'Are you going to sleep there?'

'If you will allow me to!' The Doctor glanced pointedly at the cubicle door. 'Goodnight, Miss Smith.'

Sarah took the hint and went back to her cubicle. Almost immediately Rubeish popped out of his and came over to the Doctor. 'Psst, Doctor! Shouldn't we tell the Brigadier?'

'Tell him what?'

Rubeish nodded towards Sarah. 'About *her*.'

'We can decide what to do about Miss Smith in the morning—if we're all still here. Goodnight, Professor.'

Rubeish went back into his cubicle. He sat on the end of the bed, a worried frown on his face.

Sarah sat down in her armchair, pulling a blanket over her, determined to stay awake.

Only the Doctor seemed calm and relaxed. Sprawled out in his armchair, he was dozing contentedly.

Nothing else happened for quite some time. Sarah's head nodded, and she dropped into an uneasy sleep.

Rubeish stretched out on his bed fully dressed, wondering if he ought to rouse the Brigadier and tell him about Miss Smith. He was still wondering when he too fell asleep.

In the Doctor's cubicle a valve in the rhondium sensor glowed brightly, and there was a low-pitched ringing. Instantly the Doctor sat up, awake and alert. He examined the apparatus. On a compass-type dial a needle was swinging—pointing directly at Rubeish's cubicle. The Doctor jumped up and hurried over to Rubeish's door. 'Rubeish? Rubeish!'

A peevish sleepy voice called, 'What is it? What's the matter?'

Relieved, the Doctor said, 'It's all right, just checking. Nothing to be alarmed about.'

He went to his cubicle and stood staring thoughtfully at the apparatus. Sarah appeared in the doorway. 'What's happening?'

'For a start, you're asking questions again!' The Doctor studied the compass needle. It still pointed straight towards Rubeish's cubicle—and if anything the trace was stronger. Suddenly they heard a yell and a crash—then silence.

The Doctor raced to Rubeish's door and flung it open. The cubicle was empty. A bedside lamp lay smashed upon the floor.

'He's gone,' said Sarah unbelievingly. 'But we were watching the door—and there's no other way out!'

The Doctor nodded thoughtfully. 'And he was in here a moment ago. I was speaking to him.'

Sarah noticed something on the floor and picked it up. It was Rubeish's spectacle case. She looked inside. 'Well he won't have gone far. His glasses are still here—he's blind as a bat without them.'

Sarah at his heels, the Doctor went back to his own

50

cubicle and again studied the readings on his tracking device. Shaking his head, he opened the black box and took out a bulky object like a strangely shaped torch.

'What's that?' asked Sarah.

'A black-light lamp. I'm just going to check the landing. Stay here!'

The Doctor hurried on to the landing just as two patrolling sentries appeared. 'Have you seen anyone out here?' demanded the Doctor. 'Or anything unusual?'

'No, sir. Everything's quiet.'

'Keep still!' Watched by the baffled soldiers the Doctor switched on the black-light lamp and swung it round in a slow arc. He scanned the corridor with no result, then turned his attention to the staircase leading up to the next floor. He swung the invisible beam of the lamp along it, starting at the bottom and moving it slowly upwards. As it reached the darkness at the top of the stairs a strange figure appeared. It was wearing silvery armour, with a great domed helmet.

One of the sentries gave a gasp of astonishment, swung up his sub-machine gun and fired a long raking burst. The figure vanished, and the sentries clattered up the stairs in pursuit. Shaking his head, the Doctor turned and went back into the dormitory. Heads were popping out of the cubicles, and there was a babble of confused questions.

Ignoring them, the Doctor went back into his cubicle. He studied the readings on the dial, compared them with readings on the black-light device, made a few rapid mental calculations and nodded thoughtfully. Suddenly he heard Sarah's voice. 'What happened, Doctor? What were they shooting at?'

'Shadows, I'm afraid.'

'Oh come on, Doctor. Stop treating me like a child.'

The Doctor picked up the black-light lamp. 'I can't understand why the definition was so low,' he said thoughtfully. 'Unless of course he's operating with a very weak power source at maximum range . . .' The Doctor went over to the TARDIS, opened the door with his key and went inside. He studied the instrument console, took a number of different readings, mentally compared them with those on the rhondium sensor, and gave a nod of satisfaction. He heard the Brigadier's voice. 'Doctor! Will you kindly come out of there?'

The Doctor hurried out of the TARDIS, leaving the door open behind him. The Brigadier stood waiting, immaculate as ever, despite the hour. 'Trouble, I'm afraid, Doctor. A considerable quantity of electronic equipment has vanished from the labs, and several scientists have disappeared. Everyone present in this dormitory?'

'No, Professor Rubeish is missing.' The Doctor began dismantling his tracking equipment and replacing it in the black box.

The Brigadier took off his cap, and mopped his forehead. 'Oh my giddy aunt, the Minister will go spare. Did you see anything, Doctor?'

'Yes. Something that looked like a man in armour.'

'Old-fashioned armour you mean? A ghost?'

'I very much doubt it. Sorry, Brigadier, I can't stop to explain.'

'Why not? Where are you going?'

'After Rubeish. Must get on the trail while the scent's still warm.'

'What trail? The chap's just vanished without trace.'

'Oh no he hasn't. I managed to get a fix on him—or rather on where he's been taken. You know, Brigadier, there's something very odd going on here!'

'That, Doctor, is not exactly news to me,' said the Brigadier exasperatedly. 'What's happening? How is it being done?'

'Someone's using an osmic transporter beam. But the really odd thing is, there's a time-transference factor too. It's being worked from several centuries ago!' The Doctor picked up the lamp and the black box. 'Well, I can't stay here chatting, old chap. I'm going after poor old Rubeish.'

'Doctor, I forbid you to go off in that contraption. There's no telling where you'll fetch up. Remember Metebelis Three!'

The Doctor was stung. 'I got there eventually, didn't I?'

'Eventually indeed! After detouring round most of the universe, according to Miss Grant.'

The Doctor drew a deep breath. 'Now see here, Brigadier . . .' The argument began to grow heated.

Sarah had been listening with increasing fascination. She didn't understand what the two men were arguing about—but she was growing more and more certain that she was on to the biggest story of her life. She noticed that the Doctor and the Brigadier both had their backs to the mysterious police box. Could the thing be a kind of conjuror's cabinet? Perhaps the Doctor had spirited Professor Rubeish inside. The Doctor and the Brigadier were still rowing furiously. Unnoticed, Sarah slipped past them, and into the TARDIS. 'Professor Rubeish,' she called softly, and stopped with a gasp of astonishment.

Instead of the cupboard-sized space she'd expected, she saw a large brightly-lit control room with a many-sided control console in the centre. Before she could fully take in the wonder of her surroundings, the Doctor's angry voice came from outside. 'A straight line may be the shortest distance between two points, Brigadier, but it is by no means the most interesting. Goodbye.' She heard footsteps approaching and looked round for somewhere to hide. There was a kind of cupboard set into one wall. Sarah opened it and jumped inside. She found herself in a dark, enclosed space with cloth hanging all around her. The sensation was oddly familiar. Somehow it reminded her of childhood games. She was in a wardrobe! Opening the door a crack, Sarah peered out. She saw the Doctor come into the control room, stow black box and lamp away in another wall-locker, and go to the central console. His hands moved swiftly over the controls and there was a hum of power. A transparent central column began moving up and down.

In the dormitory outside, the Brigadier heard the familiar wheezing, groaning noise as the TARDIS faded away. All that was left of the Doctor was his cloak, draped forgotten over his chair. The Brigadier sighed. 'Lord knows when I'll see him again.' He turned and marched out of the room, wondering how he was going to explain this to the Minister. Not only had he lost more scientists, he'd now lost his investigator as well . . .

6

A Shock for Sarah

Sarah crouched in the semi-darkness for what seemed a very long time, her mind whirling with wild speculations. She knew that she was in the presence of technological sophistication far beyond anything known on Earth. The wardrobe in which she was hiding was bigger than the police box appeared to be from outside, and there was that huge control room as well. Sarah began groping towards a theory. Suppose the Doctor was an alien from another planet. Suppose *he* was the one kidnapping scientists and stealing equipment, as part of some plan to spy on Earth's scientific progress?

But in that case why was he on such good terms with the Brigadier? Perhaps the Brigadier had been tricked. Sarah decided that she would get out of this incredible police box as soon as she could, leave the Research Centre, and take her discoveries to someone high up in the Government. Somehow she'd make them listen.

Sarah noticed that the central column was slowing down. The Doctor checked several readings, and then pulled a switch. The doors opened and the Doctor went outside.

Sarah forced herself to wait for a few minutes longer. Then she crossed to the control console and operated the switch she'd seen the Doctor use. To her relief, the doors started to open. Sarah ran outside—and found herself in a forest, at dawn on a summer morning. This second shock was almost too much for her. She staggered, clutching the TARDIS for support. She tried to go back inside, but the door had closed behind her, and refused to open again. She shook her head and forced down a wave of giddiness. Taking a deep breath she walked all round the police box. 'It's still only a police box—on the outside anyway,' she thought. 'I've got to find a telephone.' She stood looking round her, trying to get her bearings. The forest was thick and green and leafy, and seemed to stretch for miles. The morning sun sparkled on the dewy leaves, and the birds were singing loudly. And there was something about the air. She drew a deep breath. It was incredibly fresh and clean, as if it had never been contaminated by any kind of pollution.

Suddenly she caught a glimpse of grey stone through the trees. Some kind of building. There would be people there, and a telephone. A forest trail led straight towards the building. Sarah hurried along it as fast as she could.

The Doctor was moving in the same direction, though by a more roundabout route, and far more cautiously. He knew, as Sarah did not, that the TARDIS had travelled back in time, into England's medieval past. It was a savage, dangerous age, and the Doctor was taking no chances. If his calculations were correct, the castle he could see through the trees was the centre of the strange force that was causing scientists and equipment to disappear from twentieth-century Earth. His brief glimpse of the strange figure on the landing had given the Doctor the beginning of a theory. Now he was looking for confirmation. If his theory was correct, he was facing a savage, scientifically advanced, and utterly ruthless foe.

Hal had chosen his vantage point well. The grassy knoll gave him a clear view of the eastern battlements of

Irongron's castle. Here Irongron walked every morning, surveying his little empire and plotting fresh conquests. The distance was not too great, and if Hal was given a clear shot, this would be Irongron's final appearance. Hal had no scruples about shooting the robber down from ambush. Chivalry was something for the nobles. As far as Hal was concerned the death of Irongron would make the world a sweeter place. He strung his longbow with care, and selected a goose-feathered arrow from his quiver . . .

High on the battlements, a door opened in the little corner-turret and Irongron strode out. He took deep breaths of the clear morning air, clearing his head of the fumes of last night's wine. Bloodaxe, no lover of early rising, followed his leader on to the battlements, and stood shivering in the crisp morning air.

Irongron rested his hands on the battlements, and gazed over the forest. 'Sir Edward's castle is strong, Bloodaxe, but we know now that he has only a puny force. He stands safe within his walls. Could we but breach them . . .'

Eagerly Bloodaxe completed his leader's thought. 'We could cut down Sir Edward's men in less time than our rogues spend over breakfast!'

'Those accursed walls,' growled Irongron. He hammered a mailed fist on the stone. 'Walls like these—aye, and thicker too. But with Linx's new weapons we shall cast them down, Bloodaxe. And that will be only the first of our conquests . . .'

From below Irongron's burly figure was silhouetted clearly against the sky-line. Hal fitted the arrow to his longbow, drew it back till the goose-feather touched his ear . . .

As he loosed the arrow, a voice behind him said politely, 'Excuse me—can you tell me where to find the nearest telephone?'

Hal jumped and swung round. A slim dark maiden was staring at him. Her clothes were strange, and as far as Hal was concerned, her words were gibberish. She had spoiled his shot—and there was no time for another. Soon Irongron's men would be searching the forest. Hal turned and ran, disappearing amongst the trees.

Sarah stared after him in amazement. It was strange enough to find a sort of Robin Hood wandering about the forest. But why had the man fled at the sight of her? Puzzled, she set off for the castle.

Irongron glared at the still-quivering arrow, almost choking with indignation. It had whistled past his ear and thudded into the wooden doorway of the turret.

Bloodaxe peered over the battlements and saw two figures on the edge of the forest. 'He flees through the forest!' roared Bloodaxe. He ran down to the other side of the battlement walkway and bellowed down into the inner courtyard. 'Rouse yourself, dogs, we are attacked. Search the woods!' Baffled and sleepy, the first of Irongron's men began running for the drawbridge.

Sarah was looking at the front of the little castle. It was a picturesque enough place, she thought, like something out of a fairy story. Grey stone walls, turreted towers at each corner, rows of battlements. The little moat was dried up though, and the drawbridge seemed permanently down. There was a little gatehouse by the main entrance. Perhaps they'd have a telephone in there . . .

Suddenly a group of mail-clad men rushed out of the castle and ran towards her. Sarah stood gaping at them in astonishment. Obviously there was some sort of pageant going on, she thought. One of those re-creations of the fairs of the middle ages with jousts and tourneys and roast oxen for the tourists. 'Hey, you there,' she called. Most of the men ran straight past her, but to her astonished indignation the last two stopped and grabbed her.

'Let go of me!' yelled Sarah. 'Get off, will you? If this is some kind of joke, it isn't funny . . .'

The men weren't joking. They were dirty and unshaven and their fingers gripped her with savage force. Ignoring her attempts to break free, they dragged her across the drawbridge.

The Doctor watched all this from the edge of the woods. He'd arrived just in time to witness Sarah's capture. 'Oh no!' he thought. 'How did she get here?'

Still struggling, Sarah was dragged across the little courtyard and through an arched doorway. The Doctor heard a final yell of 'Let me go!' and she disappeared from sight.

He looked round. The rest of the guards had run straight past him and disappeared into the woods. There was no one at the gate house, and for the moment the courtyard was empty. The Doctor ran out of the forest, across the unguarded drawbridge and into the castle yard. It was a muddy, untidy place littered with bales of hay, barrels of ale and wine, farm carts and all sorts of odds and ends, most of them stolen. The Doctor ducked behind a barrel and considered his next move.

On the other side of the yard a flight of steps led down into some lower area—and someone was climbing them. The Doctor ducked down lower, and peered round the edge of the barrel. A squat figure climbed heavily up the stairs and came into the courtyard. It wore silvery armour, and a domed helmet covered its head. It was the same figure the Doctor had seen at the top of the staircase in the research centre. Not a shadowy projection this time, but solid and real, as real as the heavy wooden barrel behind which the Doctor was hiding or the muddy flagstones of the yard beneath his feet.

The figure looked round the yard as if making sure that it was alone, then raised its hands and lifted the helmet from its head. The face beneath was something out of a nightmare. The head was huge and round, emerging directly from the massive shoulders. The hairless skull was greenish-brown in colour, the eyes small and red. The little nose was a pig-like snout, the mouth long and lipless. It was a face from one of Earth's dark legends, the face of a goblin or a troll.

But the Doctor was a Time Lord and to him it meant something very different. He gave a little nod of satisfaction. 'Just as I suspected—a Sontaran!'

7

Prisoner in the Past

There was a confused shouting from outside the castle, and the noise of approaching feet. Immediately, the alien replaced its helmet and disappeared down the stairs. A group of guards came through the gate and into the yard. They had another prisoner, a tall fair-haired man dressed in green. The Doctor watched as they dragged him across the cluttered yard, through the arched doorway and into the castle. The man struggled furiously every inch of the way.

For the moment all was quiet again. A number of different doorways led off the little courtyard. Choosing one at random, the Doctor slipped into the castle.

In a corner of the great hall, two of Irongron's soldiers were putting an edge on his favourite battleaxe. One turned the handle, the other held the blade to the revolving stone. There was a shriek of stone on metal, and sparks flew into the air. Irongron watched their efforts with critical interest. 'Make it keen, you knaves—out of kindness to Sir Edward. I'd not have him feel the moment his head is parted from his shoulders.' He looked up as Bloodaxe dragged a strangely-dressed female into the hall. 'What is this?'

Sarah was still struggling wildly. 'Let me go, you great skinny oaf!'

'She was found within bowshot of the walls, Captain,' reported Bloodaxe. 'We caught another too, an archer. The men are bringing him now.'

Sarah wrenched herself free of her captor's grip. 'Idiots! Why don't you stop this ridiculous pantomine?'

Irongron chuckled. 'She spits fire, eh, Bloodaxe? Come here, girl.'

'Get lost!'

Irongron lunged forward with surprising speed and his big hand clamped round her arm, dragging her forward. He studied her for a moment, then snatched the pendant from round her neck, breaking the thin gold chain. He held it up. 'See, Bloodaxe, she wears gold!'

Sarah rubbed her neck and tried to pull away. 'That hurt, you fool.'

Irongron shook her roughly. 'You call Irongron a fool? I'll have the marrow from your bones, my pretty chicken. Where did you come from?'

Sarah said furiously, 'Look, just pack this up, will you? I'm a reporter and I'm working on a very big story—'

With a sweep of his arm, Irongron threw Sarah across to Bloodaxe, who held her firmly. 'Take her away, Bloodaxe. Put her in the dungeons, we'll question her later.'

Sarah was still more angry than frightened. 'Why don't you take off that ridiculous costume and go home to your butcher's shop? I suppose this is your big event of the year, your local historical pageant or something? I warn you, if you don't leave me alone I'm going straight to the police...'

Irongron chuckled. 'By my oath, Bloodaxe, she has a spark in her! Loose her.'

Bloodaxe released Sarah's arms, and she moved thankfully away from him. 'That's better. Now, if I can just use your telephone...'

There came the sounds of struggle from outside and a yell of rage. (Hal had managed to break free, but had soon been re-captured and pulled down.) Now, bruised

62

and bleeding, he was dragged into the hall and flung down at Irongron's feet.

'This is the dog that shot at you, Captain,' said Bloodaxe. 'See.' He pointed to Hal's bow and quiver, now held by one of the guards.

Irongron promptly kicked his captive in the ribs. 'So! You thought to kill Irongron, eh?'

'Aye,' gasped Hal. 'I would have too, but for her.' He pointed to Sarah. 'She spoiled my aim.'

Irongron kicked him again. 'Did Sir Edward send you?' He snatched up his axe and raised it menacingly. 'Speak, dog!'

'It was Lady Eleanor.'

'That narrow-hipped vixen! Make preparations for the attack, Bloodaxe. Tomorrow we dine at Sir Edward's castle.'

'Yes, Captain. What of the archer here?'

Irongron ran a grimy thumb along the edge of his axe. He tossed it to Bloodaxe. 'I leave him to you, Bloodaxe. See that you attend to him—*sharply*.'

Bloodaxe caught the axe, looking puzzled. Then a slow grin spread over his long face. 'Sharply, eh? 'Tis richly put ... A fine jest, Captain.'

Irongron gave a self-satisfied smile. 'I'm not one of your stuffy nobles, Bloodaxe, I like a bit of rough fun.'

''Tis true, Captain. Indeed you have a merry wit.' Bloodaxe nodded to the guards, and they dragged Hal away.

Sarah had been looking on in unbelieving astonishment. 'Look, please, you've had your laugh. Won't you stop it now and talk sensibly? I mean, if it's any consolation, you're scaring me out of my wits.'

Bloodaxe shook his head. 'The wench is crazed, Captain.'

'Please,' said Sarah. 'What is this place?'

Irongron bowed. 'You are in the castle of Irongron, my lady,' he said ironically. 'Few uninvited guests come here—and few of those that do come leave alive.'

Sarah said resignedly, 'All right, if you insist on playing guessing games . . . Not a village pageant then, too elaborate for that . . . Film set? No, no lights, no cameras.' She looked thoughtfully round the hall. It was filthy, dust and grime everywhere. It was furnished only with the long central table and a scattering of heavy, crudely-made stools and chairs. The table was covered with well-used metal platters and tankards, the floor strewn with dirty rushes and littered with old bones. Sarah looked at her two captors, the massive bearded leader and his lanky, fair-haired henchman. Both wore rough homespun clothing and leather topcoats studded with steel. They had swords and daggers in their belts. Their hair was long and dirty, their hands and faces grimy, and they gave off a reek of savagery, like wild beasts in a zoo. Sarah made a last desperate attempt to find some rational explanation. 'I've got it! One of those special tourist places. Medieval castle all restored to its original condition—I see you've even got a minstrels' gallery. Jolly banquets for the tourists, with authentic middle-ages food and foaming mugs of ale handed out by buxom serving wenches. That's it, isn't it?' She smiled winningly at Irongron.

Irongron said, 'You were right, Bloodaxe. The wench is crazed. A pity, she is not uncomely despite these strange clothes she wears.'

Sarah went on chattering brightly, talking to dispel her own fears. 'Mind you, I think you're overdoing things a bit. I mean, I know things were pretty scruffy in the middle ages, but really! You might leave the tourists a bit of glamour and illusion. I've never seen such a scurvy, smelly pair in my life!'

Irongron hammered the table with a huge fist. 'For pity's sake wench, stop this lunatic babbling!'

Sarah stopped. For all her protestations, she knew that this was no game or tourist pageant. This was real.

Bloodaxe whispered, 'Captain, look!'

Linx was standing in the doorway. 'Ah, Linx!' growled Irongron. 'Where are my weapons?'

'I have something to show you.'

As the Sontaran came forward, Bloodaxe edged nervously to the door. 'By your leave, Captain, I will see to the execution.'

Irongron nodded. 'Aye, and do it sharply, eh, Bloodaxe?'

'I'll have the dog fetched to the courtyard, Captain, and send word when all is ready.' Bloodaxe went out still chuckling. 'Sharply. 'Tis richly put!'

Linx looked hard at Sarah. 'What is this?'

Irongron shrugged. 'A girl, taken in the forest.'

'Girl? Ah, I see. You have two species on this planet?'

'What say you?'

'This creature is not of your kind. The hair is finer, the thorax of a different construction.'

'Hell's teeth! Have you no girls up there in the stars? No one to do the lowly work?'

'Ah, I understand. You still have a primary and secondary reproductive cycle. It is very inefficient. You should change it.'

Irongron was completely lost. Could no one talk sense this day? 'Change? Change what?'

'In the Sontaran Military Academy we have hatchings of a million cadets at each muster parade. Thus we can sustain enormous casualties and still renew our numbers.'

Irongron groaned. 'Linx, your tongue clatters worse than the wench's—'

The Sontaran touched Sarah's sleeve. 'The cloth she wears is machine-woven. This girl is not of your time.'

'Curse the girl! Show me my new weapon.'

Linx took out a metal tube and shone it into Sarah's eyes. She went rigid, staring straight ahead of her. 'Who? What? How?' snapped Linx.

She answered in a monotone. 'Sarah Jane Smith. Reporter. In a . . . machine. I did not understand it.'

'Century?'

'Twentieth.'

'Your civilisation had no conception of time-dimensional technology. Explain the machine which brought you here.'

'I cannot. It belongs to someone called Doctor John Smith.'

'Linx,' said Irongron impatiently. 'My new weapon . . .'

The Sontaran waved him away. 'Silence. This is important. The security of my mission may be threatened.' He turned back to Sarah. 'Explain this Doctor.'

'He's a scientist. He said he was interested in delta particles.'

'Ah! Is he here with you in this time zone?'

'Somewhere. I was still hiding in the machine when he left.'

Linx put the tube back in his belt. It was all becoming clear. Someone had pursued him back from the twentieth century. But how?

He became aware of Irongron's insistent voice. 'Have you done, Linx? What of my new weapon?'

Linx swung round in anger, controlling himself with an effort. He still needed the help of this primitive so he must provide the toys to keep his friendship. He took a metal box from his belt-pouch. A number of controls were set into the lid, and Linx stabbed at one with a stubby finger. There was a clang of metallic footsteps and a giant figure stalked into the hall, sword in hand. It was a knight in black armour, the helmet-visor down.

Irongron sprang to his feet, drawing his sword. 'Who are you? How dare you come in my castle?'

The figure did not move or speak.

Irongron brandished his sword. 'Speak, fellow! Answer me, or lose your head for your insolence!'

There was grim amusement in Linx's voice. 'It cannot answer you. It is a man made of iron.'

'But it walks.'

'It walks and it fights, Lord Irongron. Is it a good weapon?'

'Does it kill?'

'It does nothing else. And it cannot be killed.'

Sarah came out of her trance with a start. She tried to remember what had happened but the last few minutes were a blank. She was sure only of one thing. She wanted to get right away from this terrible place.

Without moving her head, she glanced around her. The black bearded man and a strange squat-looking knight were studying what appeared to be a suit of black armour. The others had all gone. Slowly, Sarah began to edge towards the door . . .

8

The Robot Knight

Irongron looked admiringly at the huge black figure of the robot knight. 'By Heaven, Linx! Can you make me more of these?'

'If you wish.'

'With such soldiers, I could conquer the world!'

'When I have left this primitive planet it will amuse me to think of it under the rule of King Irongron. Provide me with everything I ask and I will make you many of these fighting robots.'

'It is a bargain! By my sword, Linx, I little thought when I first saw you that I should come to love you as a brother. Now, quickly, show me how your iron man works.'

Linx looked round. 'Wait! The female creature has gone.'

Engrossed in his new toy, Irongron had no time to worry about stray prisoners, especially mad ones. 'She'll not creep far before one of my guards catches her tail.' He looked eagerly at the black knight. 'Make it walk, Linx. Make it fight!'

Linx touched the hand control, and the knight began stalking towards them. He adjusted another control and it raised its sword. The knight marched forward chopping up with its sword, up, down, up, down in mechanical fury. It stumbled into a heavy wooden chair and shattered it to matchwood with a series of smashing blows.

Irongron's eyes shone. He saw an army of these metal knights, smashing down all who stood in their way, bringing the whole country, the whole world under the rule of King Irongron!

Sarah got clear of the hall without being seen, and even managed to reach a door that led to the courtyard. Two of Irongron's men were lounging just beside it, and she'd been forced to turn back into the castle. Now she was hurrying along one of the back corridors, hoping to find another way out. She came to a T-junction, hesitated, turned left—and ran straight into the Doctor. For a moment they stared at each other in astonishment. Sarah spun round, and fled.

The Doctor hurried after her, yelling, 'Miss Smith! Hey, Sarah, come back!' When he reached the corner she was nowhere in sight. 'Stupid girl,' he muttered. He was about to go in search of her when he heard footsteps and ducked back round the corner.

Two mailed men were dragging a third between them. He was dressed in Lincoln green, and his arms were bound behind him. Behind the little party marched another man. There was a huge two-handed axe over his shoulder. The little group went straight on down the corridor, and out through a door at the far end. The Doctor waited for a moment and followed them.

Higher up the corridor was an alcove, curtained by a musty tapestry. The tapestry stirred and Sarah emerged from hiding. She crept cautiously after the Doctor.

Bloodaxe surveyed his arrangements with pride. After all, if you were going to have an execution you might as well do it in style. Some people disposed of unwanted prisoners with a quick stab in the back, but Bloodaxe took pride in doing these things properly.

He'd even had a proper execution-block set up in the middle of the yard. He waved his hand. Hal was dragged forward, forced to his knees, then thrust down on to the block, his head projecting over the edge. Bloodaxe spat on his palms, hefted his axe and took a few practice swings. Then he shouldered the axe again, waiting for the arrival of Irongron. The Captain always liked a good execution.

Hiding behind an ox-cart, the Doctor looked on in horror. He knew he had to do something to help—but what? The yard was full of villainous-looking men-at-arms, waiting to see the fun—and he was unarmed.

The Doctor looked higher. A kind of walkway ran along the top of the walls surrounding the courtyard. It was patrolled by a solitary sentry armed with a cross-bow. He was supposed to be looking outwards into the forest, but instead he was gazing down into the yard. A flight of steps in the corner led up to the walkway. The Doctor started working his way towards it.

Sarah was peeping round the edge of the door, trying to tell herself it was all a bit of mock-medieval fun. Somewhere there was a hidden camera, and soon they'd all pack up and have a cup of tea. But in her heart she knew that this was no joke. Somehow she'd been plunged into the brutal realities of history—and soon a real head would roll across the muddy cobblestones of the yard. She saw Irongron appear in the main door-way. Bloodaxe nodded to his Captain, took the axe from his shoulder and raised it high . . .

'Stay, Bloodaxe!' bellowed Irongron.

Bloodaxe arrested the axe inches from Hal's neck and stared indignantly at Irongron, who was grinning savagely. 'I have devised better sport for us.' He strode out into the courtyard followed by a man-at-arms carrying Hal's bow and quiver. Irongron went up to the block and gazed down at Hal. 'Will you fight for your life, fellow?'

Hal struggled to his knees. 'I'll fight any man.'

'Then stand against Irongron's champion!'

There was a strange metal device in Irongron's hand. He touched it—and a giant knight in black armour marched stiffly into the yard.

Bloodaxe stared at the newcomer. 'Who is this, Captain?' he whispered.

Irongron was rocking with suppressed mirth. 'You'll see good sport now, Bloodaxe. Release the dog!'

Bloodaxe pulled Hal to his feet and severed his bonds. 'Give him his bow.'

The man-at-arms passed Hal his bow and quiver. Hal took them, hardly able to believe his eyes.

Bloodaxe sidled up to Irongron. ''Tis not fair combat, Captain, knight against bowman. At this range, the arrows will pierce the armour with ease.' It was true enough. At many a battle the armoured chivalry of France had been brought down by English bowmen.

Irongron waved him away. He looked at Hal. 'Are you game, fellow?'

'That I am,' said Hal grimly. He notched an arrow to his bow, and stepped back to get a clear aim at the motionless black figure.

'Your freedom if you kill him,' promised Irongron. 'Stand back, all of you.'

Hurriedly the spectators widened their circle. Irongron touched his control again. The black knight strode jerkily forward, sword raised high.

Hal drew back the bow-string, aimed and fired, all in one smooth motion. The arrow whistled across the courtyard and thudded into the weak point where helmet joins neck, transfixing the black knight through the throat.

Without breaking step, the knight came jerkily on.

71

There was a gasp of unbelieving astonishment from the spectators. 'See, Captain, he still moves!' breathed Bloodaxe. Irongron gave him a slap on the back that almost floored him, and exploded with a bellow of laughter. 'Aye, that he does, good Bloodaxe! That he does.'

No one was more astonished than Hal. Despite his surprise, he had fitted another arrow to his bow. He fired again. This time the arrow pierced the black knight's breastplate directly over the heart. Yet still his uncanny foe stalked towards him. Hal jumped back as the black knight's sword whistled down. Fumbling for a third arrow he backed away. The black knight stalked after him.

The Doctor was at the top of the stairs by now. The sentry was leaning over the courtyard, transfixed by the astonishing spectacle below. The Doctor began edging towards him.

Hal fired again, and another arrow pierced the black knight through the heart. Yet still it came on. Panic-stricken, Hal leaped back—and stumbled over an abandoned wagon-wheel. He tripped and fell. The black knight loomed over him, sword raised high for the kill—and waited.

The Doctor lowered the unconscious sentry to the ground and straightened up, crossbow in hand. He took careful aim. He'd had lessons from William Tell once, but that had been a long time ago . . .

As Irongron was about to transmit the instruction for the killing blow a crossbow-bolt smashed the control-unit from his hand. Rubbing numbed fingers he glared angrily round the courtyard. 'What rogue did that?' He looked up and saw a tall figure running along the wall. Suddenly Bloodaxe gave a shout of alarm. 'Guard yourself, Captain.'

The robot knight was staggering towards them, sword flailing like the arms of a windmill.

Irongron lugged out his own sword just in time to parry the first smashing blow—and found himself fighting for his life.

The Doctor looked down from the wall and smiled grimly. This was even better than he'd hoped. The shattering of the control unit had sent the robot berserk, and it was providing the diversion he so desperately needed. Meanwhile Hal had taken his opportunity and was running towards the open gate. But two of Irongron's men were blocking his way. Hal changed direction, and a door close by swung open.

'This way,' called Sarah. Hal ran through the door and it closed behind him.

In the courtyard, battle was still raging. Several crossbow-bolts had now joined Hal's arrows, but the robot seemed quite unaffected. Somehow it had fixed on Irongron as its target, and pursued him with remorseless fury. It took all of Irongron's strength and skill to parry the rain of blows, and he staggered back and back, grunting with fatigue . . .

It was the faithful Bloodaxe who came to his Captain's aid. Snatching up the axe that had been intended for Hal, he leaped boldly forward and swung the axe in a whistling arc that lopped the black knight's head from its shoulders. The helmet rolled across the courtyard, and the headless figure reeled, changed direction, staggered into a corner and stood slashing blindly at the stone wall.

Irongron drew a deep sobbing breath, and mopped his brow. 'By heaven, Bloodaxe, 'tis like a tin tadpole. Cut off its head and yet it wriggles. It nearly slew *me*! I will have words with Linx about this!'

Irongron stamped off through the arched doorway,

followed by Bloodaxe and most of the men-at-arms. One or two remained, grouped round the robot, watching as its still-slashing sword struck sparks from the stones. Finally, they too lost interest and drifted away.

For a moment the courtyard was deserted. The side door opened, Sarah and Hal looked cautiously out. Seeing the empty courtyard, they ran swiftly and silently across the drawbridge and disappeared into the forest.

From his place on the wall, the Doctor watched them go. Now, if those two would only keep out of his way, perhaps he could find out what was going on in this very strange castle . . .

9

Linx's Slaves

Linx stood helmetless in the doorway of his scout ship and stared round the huge underground store-room. All around him slave-scientists were busy at their tasks, repairing delicate circuits, forging new ones where the damage was too great. Grey-faced, red-eyed, stumbling with exhaustion, they worked without cease. Yet still Linx was not satisfied. So much still to be done with these crude, improvised tools and clumsy workers. Would he never be free of this primitive planet? He looked up angrily as someone began hammering on the door.

(Absorbed with his never-ending problems, Linx had failed to notice that a figure had appeared on the other side of the window grille. The Doctor peered into the room, looking at the strange equipment, the toiling figures, the Sontaran scout-ship in one corner, and knew that his search was over. The metal grille covering the window was loose in its frame of stonework. The Doctor gave an experimental heave. The grille shifted a little. He heaved again, then ducked swiftly back out of sight at the sudden hammering on the door.)

'Linx,' bellowed an angry voice. 'Come out, Linx, you mongrel toad! I have a bone to pick with you!' The door shivered under a massive blow.

Linx's little red eyes glowed with anger. 'I am occupied, Irongron.'

'Out this minute, dog, or I shall burst down the door.'

Contemptuously Linx turned away. There was a shattering crash, the lock burst open, and the door slammed back against the wall. Irongron stood framed in the doorway, sword in hand. He opened his mouth to bellow a threat—and the breath choked in his throat as he saw the Sontaran's face for the very first time. He staggered back, his left hand making a clumsy attempt at the sign of the cross.

Linx said ironically, 'Well? What were you in such haste to say to me?' Irongron gulped. The Sontaran's thin lips twitched. 'I told you that you might not find my face pleasing.'

Irongron rubbed his eyes with a massive paw. 'Aye, and never was truer word spoken. Are they all as fair of face beyond the stars?'

'The variety of sentient life-forms is infinite. Do you think your primitive features are pleasing to me? What is it that you want?'

Irongron remembered his grievance. 'This cursed iron warrior of yours ...'

'You are pleased with it? I can make you many more, if you keep our bargain.'

'More!' bellowed Irongron. 'I tell you, Linx, with allies such as that, I have small need of enemies. The creature nearly had my life. We riddled it with arrows, and Bloodaxe smote off its head. Yet still it sought to slay me!'

'The measure of a weapon is the skill of the man who handles it. Your sword is useless to one who does not understand how to wield it. You must have mismanaged the hand control.'

Irongron stared at him. In the business of actually dealing with the robot, he had temporarily forgotten how the crisis had come about. 'Some knave smote the control from my hands with a crossbow-bolt. Sir Edward must have sent men to rescue his archer. Your iron man became crazed, Linx. It tried to slay us all!'

'Perhaps the hand control itself is a weakness,' said Linx thoughtfully. 'I will build you another, better warrior, Irongron, one that will obey your voice.'

Irongron grunted. 'First help me kill the one I have now. It still struggles to slay my knaves.'

The Sontaran gave a rasping sigh. 'It cannot be killed, Irongron, it was never alive. Come, I will de-activate it. Then perhaps you will give me peace to continue my work.' He led Irongron out of the chamber.

A few minutes' work on the mortar with his sonic screwdriver, followed by some good old-fashioned heaving, enabled the Doctor to loosen the iron grille and pull it aside. He squeezed through the gap and dropped down into the room.

The Doctor stood for a moment looking at the silent, busy figures at the tables. They went on with their work, ignoring him. He saw the computer standing against the wall, the Sontaran scout ship in the far corner. How on earth had they got it down here? They must have dragged the little ship in with ropes and pulleys, inch by inch. The Doctor wondered how the Sontaran had persuaded his ally to undertake such a colossal task. As he looked round the room, his eye fell on the answer. Guns! A pile of them lay on one of the wooden tables. The Doctor picked one up. It was a crude but efficient percussion weapon, hundreds of years before its time. 'Insanity,' he murmured. 'Absolute insanity!' A white-coated figure came up to the table and deposited an armful of newly-assembled rifles with the others. Suddenly the Doctor realised that he knew the man—they'd met briefly at the research centre. 'Professor Morrison!' he called. Ignoring him the man stumbled away. Another scientist detached himself from the rest, groping his way blindly along the wall, and he too was familiar. 'Rubeish!'

Rubeish came to a halt, peering about like an old mole disturbed in its tunnel. 'What? Who's that?'

'It's the Doctor. We were in the same dormitory at the Research Centre.'

'Oh my dear fellow,' said the old man sympathetically. 'Got you too, has he?'

'Not exactly. What's happened to all these people, Rubeish?'

'Hypnotised, then programmed to work,' said Rubeish promptly. 'Rotten company. Can't get a word out of them.'

'You seem to be all right.'

'Didn't work with me,' said Rubeish proudly. 'He doesn't know, of course. I keep out of his way, join in here and there and he thinks I'm like the others. I was too strong-minded for him.'

The Doctor looked at the old man's squinting eyes. 'Too short-sighted, more like it. He must have used some kind of ocular device. Do you realise where you are, old chap?'

'Some kind of castle, I suspect. I was feeling the carving of these columns. Astonishingly well-preserved.'

'You're in a castle all right. But do you realise the time?'

'Still morning, is it? We haven't had breakfast yet. He doesn't feed us much, you know. Once a day, if we're lucky.'

The Doctor took a deep breath. 'Steel yourself, Professor, this is going to be a shock to you. You've been brought back to the middle ages!'

Rubeish blinked. 'How very interesting. I've always believed that the possibility of time travel should never have been dismissed so arrogantly by Professor Crab- shaw and his cronies. In fact, my dear Doctor—'

The Doctor had no time for scientific discussions. 'Some other time, old chap. We've got to get you away before that Sontaran returns.'

'Oh not yet, Doctor, surely? There's most interesting work being done here, you know. I only wish I could see it all properly.'

'Your life is in danger here. I must insist that we leave!'

Obstinately Rubeish shook his head. 'You can go if you wish, but I'm staying. Go on, be off with you, and leave me alone!'

Huffily the old man waved the Doctor away. The Doctor looked at him in some indignation. Was this any way to treat a rescuer? It would be hard enough to get Rubeish clear of the castle if he co-operated, impossible if he was going to struggle ...

The Doctor hesitated a moment too long. Suddenly the Sontaran was in the doorway, covering him with a stubby metal tube that the Doctor recognised as a ray- gun. 'Do not move!' he rasped, and came slowly down the stairs. 'You are the one known as the Doctor?'

'You know who I am?'

'I have been expecting you. Why did you follow me to this time zone?'

'To prevent your interference with the development of Earth. Surely you realise the harm you'll cause?'

'This primitive planet and its affairs are of no im- portance to me.'

The Doctor nodded grimly. 'I should have expected that reaction. A typically Sontaran attitude.'

Linx was stung by the contempt in the Doctor's

79

voice. 'I have only one concern, Doctor, to complete the repairs to my space ship and return to the glorious war that is my destiny. Nothing must interfere with that—nothing and nobody!'

Linx raised his weapon and fired. A red glow flickered round the Doctor's body. He twisted for a moment in its glare, and crashed to the ground.

10

Irongron's Wizard

Sarah finished her bread and cheese and washed it down with the last of the wine. She gave a sigh of content, and looked up at her host and hostess. 'Thanks. I really needed that.'

'Now, child,' said Lady Eleanor firmly. 'Tell us who you are, and where you are from.'

This was the moment Sarah had been dreading. After their escape from Irongron's castle, Hal had led her on a long forced march through the woods, keeping well away from all the roads. They had come at last to this other castle, and Hal had taken her before his lord and lady. They had treated her kindly enough, but she knew they were expecting explanations. 'I don't think I can,' said Sarah helplessly. 'It's all too complicated.'

Hal was standing respectfully behind Sir Edward's chair. 'I can vouch for her, my lord. Without her help I would not be here.'

'Her manner of dress is strange,' said Edward thoughtfully. 'And her manner of speech.'

'There is much that is strange at Irongron's castle, my lord. I told you of the knight that fought on when he should have been dead. And while I was held captive, one of the guards boasted that Irongron has a wizard from the stars who makes magic weapons for him.'

Sir Edward nodded. 'It does not surprise me that one so evil seeks the aid of devils and magicians.'

Sarah couldn't keep quiet any longer. 'I can tell you who's helping him—and it's no magician. It's an eccentric scientist called the Doctor.'

Lady Eleanor said sharply. 'Who is this Doctor? What do you know of him?'

'You won't find it easy to believe this—I can hardly believe it myself. I come from another place and another time—a time where they have a kind of knowledge that would seem like magic to you.'

'And who brought you here?'

'The Doctor did—though he didn't mean to. I was suspicious of him, and stowed away—hid, in a kind of machine. Irongron's men caught me and took me to his castle.'

Sir Edward buried his face in his hands. 'Madness! Sorcery and witchcraft!'

Sarah stumbled on with her explanation. 'Scientists, wizards if you like, are being brought here from the place I come from. I believe the Doctor is handing them over to Irongron. He came straight here—and I saw him wandering round Irongron's castle.'

Lady Eleanor was struggling to understand. 'What does Irongron want with these stolen wizards?'

It was Hal who answered. 'He will force them to make him strange weapons, lady, like the knight that cannot be killed. Irongron thinks only of wars and conquest.'

'True enough, Hal,' said Sir Edward. 'And anything that makes Irongron strong can work only to our harm. Who knows what sorceries he may now have at his command?'

Sarah was thinking aloud. 'I'm sure the Doctor is the key to it all. He was there when the scientists were taken, and he has a machine that travels through time. It must be him. Somehow we've got to stop him.'

Sir Edward shook his head. 'If he is Irongron's ally, he is safe in Irongron's castle. There is nothing we can do.'

'Nonsense. There's always something you can do. It's just a matter of working out what it is! The first thing to do is get the Doctor away from Irongron.'

Sir Edward looked up. 'And force him to make his magic for me? A good thought, but how could it be done?'

'All it needs is a sort of commando raid. Wait till it gets dark, then knock out the sentries, rush into the castle, grab the Doctor and away. You've got soldiers here, haven't you?'

Sir Edward sighed. 'No more than a handful. Old men and boys for the most part.'

'I'll go, my lord,' said Hal eagerly. 'I have scores to settle with Irongron.'

As always when faced with a difficult decision, Sir Edward turned to his wife. 'It is a bold plan, Edward,' she said gently. 'And this is a time for boldness.'

'Perhaps so . . . if it is not a trap. Can we trust this witch-maiden?'

'I'm not a witch,' said Sarah indignantly. 'And I'm on your side.'

'Could you tell Hal what this Doctor looks like?' asked Lady Eleanor.

'Tell him? I'll show him. You don't think I'm staying behind do you?'

Lady Eleanor smiled tolerantly. 'This is men's work, my dear. It is a woman's place to wait.'

'Not any more,' said Sarah firmly. 'Not where I come from. I'm going on the raid, and that's that.' She looked down at her bedraggled clothes. 'Do you think you could lend me something to wear? I think men's clothes would be best.'

Lady Eleanor was too shocked to reply.

The Doctor opened his eyes and saw the ogreish face of

Linx staring down at him. Painfully he got to his feet. Linx watched him, ray gun in hand. 'You recover quickly, Doctor.' He gestured with the stubby weapon. 'I could easily have killed you by using full power.'

'Why didn't you?'

'I require you alive. A brain of your capacity can be of use to me.'

The Doctor rubbed his aching head, reflecting that at the moment his brain wouldn't be much use to anybody.

'Thank you,' he said politely.

The little red eyes studied him. 'You are not of this planet, I think. How came you to be here?'

'Just a tourist. I quite like it here, actually.'

'This mud-speck in space?'

The Doctor smiled. 'Perhaps you haven't seen it at its best.'

'It is primitive,' said the Sontaran dismissively. 'It has no military value, no strategic significance. Therefore it is worthless.'

'More Sontaran philosophy? You are a Sontaran warrior, aren't you?'

'I am Commander Linx, Fifth Sontaran Army Space Corps.'

'And why are you here? What has the perpetual war between Sontarans and Rutans to do with Earth?'

'An emergency landing. I was on a reconnaissance mission when I was attacked by a squadron of Rutan fighters.' Linx didn't care to dwell on his near-defeat. 'So, Doctor, you have heard of my race?'

'Unfortunately.'

'I overlook the insult—for the moment. What is your native planet?'

'Gallifrey. I am a Time Lord.'

'Ah yes. A race of great technical achievement,

84

lacking the morale to withstand a really determined assault.'

The Doctor said angrily. 'Oh you think so, do you? Well, just let me tell you—'

'I am only a lowly field commander, Doctor. I quote from the reports of our military intelligence.'

'You'd be well advised never to put that particular evaluation to the test,' warned the Doctor grimly.

'My ambition at the moment, Doctor, is limited to re-joining my squadron. You can be of great value to me. You can help to rebuild my ship.'

The Doctor looked at the toiling figures all around. 'You seem to have acquired a lot of help already.'

'Primitives,' said Linx contemptuously. 'I only had enough osmic power to reach the Twentieth Century.'

'Where you stole the materials and the skilled helpers you couldn't find here?'

'I took what I could find. The work goes slowly, Doctor, slowly.'

Linx raised the ray gun menacingly. 'Now take that seat, there before the computer console.' The Doctor obeyed. Projecting from the computer was a flexible arm, with a gleaming metal helmet on the end. 'Everything is ready for you, Doctor,' said Linx sardonically. He swung the helmet down, fitted it over the Doctor's head and began adjusting controls on the computer keyboard.

'You're interfering with human history,' said the Doctor desperately. 'You're going to do their culture incalculable damage.'

Linx went on with his work. 'I have no interest in human culture.'

'These humans have got to be allowed to develop at their own pace. At this period they're only a few steps away from barbarism.'

85

Linx ignored him. 'Your task is to monitor progress rates on the input circuits and adjust the programme accordingly. It is concentrated and monotonous work.' He flicked a switch and stepped back. 'Now I must leave you for a time. Later I will have more complex tasks for you.'

The Doctor raised his voice in a final appeal. 'This is a war-like species, Linx, like your own. Give them breech-loading rifles now and they'll have atomic weapons by the seventeenth century. They'll have the capability to destroy their own planet before they're civilised enough to handle it . . .'

Blue sparks crackled around the helmet and a stab of pain lanced through the Doctor's brain.

Linx smiled. 'I omitted to tell you, Doctor, there is a built-in punishment circuit. You will find it pays to concentrate on the task I have given you.'

The Doctor read the symbols flashing across the screen in front of him, made a rapid calculation and punched out his reply on the keyboard. The crackling ceased, and the pain died down.

'Excellent, Doctor. You need not suffer—as long as you work. Oh and one final warning. Do not attempt to leave the console—or the helmet will deliver a shock severe enough to kill you.' Linx gathered up an armful of rifles from the table, climbed the stairs and disappeared.

The sentry strolled slowly along the torch-lit walkway, and paused to peer down at the dark forest. Everything was quiet. No reason why it shouldn't be, of course. Sir Edward was the only enemy within range, and he would never dare to attack . . . He was about to resume his patrol when Hal sprang suddenly over the battlements and bore him to the ground.

Hal checked that the rope and the grappling hook were still holding firmly, then leaned over the battlements and waved to Sarah, who began climbing quickly up the rope. She was wearing boy's clothes now—a doublet and hose that had belonged to Sir Edward's missing squire. Hal helped her over the battlements. 'I still say this is no work for womenfolk,' he whispered.

'I'm the only one who knows what the Doctor looks like,' said Sarah. 'Besides, I wouldn't have missed this for anything.' She winced as Hal grabbed the body of the sentry and heaved it over the battlements.

Hal straightened up. 'Come then, let us go and look for Irongron's wizard.'

Sarah nodded towards the keep, the square tower that held most of the castle's rooms. 'He'll probably be in the main hall with Irongron. If we work our way along the outside, we can look in through the windows.'

Quietly they moved away.

Irongron looked exultantly at the pile of rifles on the table. He snatched one up and weighed it in his hands. 'By heaven, these are more to my taste than your murderous iron man, good Linx.'

Linx resented the implication that his robot had been a total failure. 'That was a preliminary experimental model. Now I will make you a better fighting robot for your armies.'

Irongron turned to Bloodaxe. 'Take these rifles to the men. I will come soon and teach their use.'

'Aye, Captain.' Bloodaxe began gathering up the guns.

'At dawn tomorrow, we march on Sir Edward's castle,' said Irongron happily. 'By sunset, he and his men will be feeding the crows!'

(Outside the great hall, Hal and Sarah were clinging to the chinks in the rough stonework just below the window. They peered over the window-ledge just in time to see Bloodaxe gather up the rifles, and to hear Irongron's threat. Hal looked at Sarah, and gestured urgently downwards. Quickly they began climbing down to the ground.)

The Doctor sat at the keyboard, controlling the flow of work through the computer. In response to each flow of symbols he punched in new instructions, which were transmitted directly to the brains of Linx's slaves. Thanks to the capacity of his Time Lord brain he could handle this complicated task with only a small part of his attention—the rest was directed to finding some means of escape.

Unfortunately, he couldn't seem to think of one. He couldn't leave the keyboard without being electrocuted by the helmet—unless, that is, he could switch off the mind-link. But the control switch was out of his reach, unless he left the keyboard. And he couldn't leave the keyboard without getting electrocuted . . .

The Doctor's mind went round and round this problem for a very long time as it grew dark in the underground workshop. Lights came on—installed by Linx no doubt. At last he decided the problem was insoluble—unless, that is, he could introduce some new element into the equation. A kind of random factor . . .

Suddenly the random factor came stumbling towards him. 'Professor Rubeish!' he called. 'Over here!' The old man wandered up.

'Is that you, Doctor? I thought you were going to leave.'

'Change of plan, old chap. I wonder if you could help me?'

Rubeish peered short-sightedly at him. 'Are you wearing a hat?'

'Can you feel that panel just behind you, Rubeish? There are three switches on it.'

Rubeish turned round, groping vaguely. 'Dangerous, wearing hats,' he grumbled. 'Overheats the brain.' His fingers brushed the panel. 'Yes, I've got it.'

'Good. Now, just turn the left-hand switch, will you?'

Rubeish fumbled at the panel. 'Always thought that was why judges were so peculiar, you know. It's those wigs they wear . . .' He found a switch and flicked it.

There was a crackle of sparks from the helmet, and the Doctor's body convulsed. 'Turn it off,' he yelled, 'that's the pain stimulator!'

Rubeish flicked the switch, and the Doctor relaxed. 'Sorry,' said Rubeish apologetically. 'Wish I'd brought my glasses.'

'So do I,' said the Doctor feelingly. 'Now, try again, would you, old chap? The left-hand switch, please.'

'Oh, *this* one,' Rubeish flicked another switch. Nothing happened. 'Is that the one?'

'I sincerely hope so.' Cautiously the Doctor slid his head from under the helmet. Still nothing happened. With a sigh of relief he got to his feet and stretched. 'Thank you, Professor. Will you excuse me? I must be off.'

Rubeish had been hoping for a cosy chat. 'Where are you off to now?' he demanded peevishly.

'There's a girl I've got to find. I'll see you later—I hope!' The Doctor ran up the steps.

Rubeish turned away. 'A girl? Should have thought he was a bit old for that. Ah well!' He pottered off to see what they were doing at the nearest workbench.

The Doctor went up the steps, along the gloomy

corridor, turned a corner, and walked straight into Irongron and Bloodaxe. 'Good evening,' said the Doctor politely. Irongron lunged at him. The Doctor shoved him aside, tripped him neatly, and ran for his life.

Furiously, Irongron picked himself up. 'Call the guards!' he yelled. 'Bring torches! After him!' Followed by the bewildered Bloodaxe, he set off in pursuit.

There followed a brief game of hide and seek through the darkness of the castle corridors. The Doctor was quicker-moving than his pursuers, but Irongron's yells brought more and more guards to join in the chase.

The Doctor dodged, ran, and dodged again, until at last he managed to reach a door that led to the courtyard. It was in semi-darkness, lit here and there by flickering torches. He ran out into the open and made a dash for the drawbridge.

Irongron was close behind him. 'Seize him, you knaves,' he roared. 'Pull the dog down!'

The Doctor ran to and fro like a rabbit trapped in a cornfield. He ducked in and out of cover, hurdled over obstacles, sent torch-waving men-at-arms reeling with the speed of his flight. But the space was too enclosed, and his hunters too many. He was brought down at last, tripped by a pike thrust between his legs. The Doctor crashed to the ground and Irongron pounded up to him.

'He who strikes Irongron—dies!' he roared, and raised his sword.

The Rescue

Hal and Sarah were on the battlements when the commotion broke out in the yard below. Once they'd overheard Irongron's plans, Hal had insisted on abandoning the hunt for the Doctor and returning to warn his master.

From their vantage point on the walkway they saw the Doctor hunted to and fro, saw him tripped by the pike, saw Irongron run to stand over him.

'Look,' whispered Hal. 'Irongron seeks to slay his wizard!'

Sarah grabbed his arm. 'Quick, Hal, do something! We need the Doctor alive!'

Hal stepped back, fitted an arrow to his bow. As Irongron's sword flashed down Hal fired—and missed.

Missed Irongron, that is—by a freak chance the arrow struck the hilt of Irongron's sword, sending it flying from his grasp. Instantly the Doctor was up and running once more.

He heard a voice call, 'Over here, Doctor!' and saw Sarah at the top of the walkway. He ran for the stairs, men-at-arms close on his heels. As he ran, the Doctor was looking for something to delay his pursuers. There was a stack of hay-bales near the bottom of the stairs and a torch burning in a wall-bracket nearby. The Doctor heaved a couple of bales across the bottom of the stairway, tossed the torch on top of them and sprinted up the stairs.

The dry straw caught immediately, and the blazing hay formed a fiery barrier across the bottom of the steps.

Irongron's men struggled to heave the burning bales aside, coughing and choking in the smoke. The Doctor ran up on to the battlements, where Hal and Sarah were waiting. Out of breath as he was, he managed to say politely. 'Many thanks, Miss Smith. A most timely rescue.'

'It isn't a rescue, Doctor,' said Sarah grimly. There was another arrow in Hal's bow, and it was aimed at the Doctor's heart. Sarah led him to where the rope hung from the grappling hook. 'Now, down the rope please, Doctor. And don't try to run.'

The Doctor decided to save the explanations for later. He swung his legs over the battlements and slid down the rope.

Linx stood glaring at the empty computer console. The Doctor had escaped. But how? He glared suspiciously round at the other prisoners, all working meekly at their appointed tasks.

Angrily Linx turned and went up the steps. As soon as he was out of sight, Rubeish detached himself from a group of workers and groped his way to another bench. He picked up a piece of clear plastic and resumed his task. Professor Rubeish had decided it was time he could see what was going on. He was grinding the piece of plastic into a lens . . .

Irongron glared broodingly into his pot of wine. 'The fellow has the gall of a camel and the cunning of a fox!'

'You shall be revenged, Captain,' said Bloodaxe consolingly. 'He must be one of Sir Edward's men and not even a rat shall escape Sir Edward's castle alive once we attack tomorrow!'

'On my oath, Bloodaxe, once that fellow is in my hands I shall chop him so fine not even a sparrow shall fill its beak at one peck!' Cheered by this grisly threat, Irongron took another swig of wine, and looked up as Linx marched into the hall and stood before him.

'My prisoner has disappeared. Order a search!'

Irongron grunted, in no mood to take orders from Linx. 'If one of your whey-faced ninnies is loose, then find him yourself. My men need rest. We march on Sir Edward's castle at dawn.'

'This is a special prisoner, Irongron. I insist on a search. The Doctor is of great value to me. While he is at large, I am in danger.'

Irongron turned away, reaching for the wine jug. 'Do not trouble me now, little toad—or you will feel an axe in your skull.'

Bloodaxe said, 'Captain, I heard someone call "Doctor" when we were at that fellow's heels.'

Irongron looked up. 'Linx, is this Doctor of yours a longshanked knave, with a mighty nose?'

'That is how he might appear to human eyes,' said the Sontaran impatiently.

'Then he is no longer in the castle. Sir Edward sent a raiding party to rescue him.'

'He has escaped?'

Irongron tapped the hilt of his sword. 'Aye—but not for long!'

As he waited in Sir Edward's chamber, with Hal on guard at the door, the Doctor looked round admiringly. A better class of castle altogether, this. The tapestries were clean and fresh, and so were the rushes on the floor.

'Very nice,' he said admiringly. 'You have been getting round, Sarah. Are you on visiting terms with all the local nobility?'

Sarah frowned. 'Doctor, I think it's time we got a few things straight . . .'

'I'm afraid you're going to be awfully confused if you want me to explain the TARDIS.'

'The TARDIS?'

'My police box. You stowed away in it, I imagine?'

A little embarrassed, Sarah said, 'We'll come to that later. What I want to know is, why are you helping Irongron?'

'My dear girl, I'm not helping him. Linx is. I'm trying to stop him.'

'Linx?'

'Perhaps you haven't met him yet. Nasty, brutish and short just about sums him up.'

'There was a strange-looking knight with Irongron when I was first captured,' said Sarah slowly. 'I think he hypnotised me or something.'

'That was Linx. He'd have looked even stranger if he hadn't been wearing space armour. He comes from a planet where gravity is many times that of Earth.'

Sarah said wonderingly, 'Someone from another planet . . . How do I know you're telling the truth?'

'I never lie,' said the Doctor indignantly. 'Well, hardly ever. Have you heard of UNIT?'

'The United Nations Intelligence Task Force? They were in charge of security at the Research Centre. Are you saying you work for them?'

'Purely in an advisory capacity. The Brigadier asked me to look into this business of the missing scientists.'

'I thought *you* were responsible for that.'

The Doctor sighed. 'My dear girl, do I look the sort of person who goes about kidnapping scientists?' Sarah didn't answer. Looking a little hurt the Doctor went on, 'Linx has been bringing them back here to staff his workshop. Now I have to find a way of returning them to their own time.'

They were interrupted by the arrival of Sir Edward and Lady Eleanor, who came into the room rather warily, as if expecting their new guest to disappear in a puff of blue smoke. 'This is the magician?' asked Sir Edward cautiously.

'My lady, my lord.' The Doctor produced his most elaborate bow. 'It's a privilege and a pleasure to be amongst civilised people once more.'

Sir Edward said wryly, 'A courtly rogue, at least.'

Lady Eleanor came straight to the point. 'Is he willing to change his allegiance and serve Sir Edward instead of Irongron?'

Sarah looked a little embarrassed. 'There seems to have been a bit of a mix-up. He says he wasn't serving Irongron at all. There's another stranger at the castle. Someone called Linx.'

'There is indeed,' said the Doctor. 'And he's your enemy, I assure you, not me. The most sensible thing would be for us all to join forces.'

Sir Edward looked helplessly at Sarah. 'What say you? Does he speak the truth?'

'I'm not sure. I suppose I could have been wrong—or he could just be changing sides to save his own skin.'

Lady Eleanor took her husband aside. 'These wizards and warlocks were ever a treacherous breed. We had best be wary of him.'

Sir Edward made his decision. 'Perhaps so—yet we need allies. Doctor, I shall spare your life if you cast your spells and incantations to help me against Irongron. Refuse and you die.'

The Doctor smiled. 'You offer a restricted choice.

But there's no need for threats. My services are at your disposal—such as they are.'

'Good. Serve me straight, Doctor, and I shall reward you well.'

For some time now Hal had been bursting with impatience. 'Forgive me, my lord, but are you not forgetting the news I brought you? Irongron plans to march on us at dawn. This we heard from his own lips.'

Sir Edward sank slowly into his chair. 'Aye, so you said. And we cannot stand against him.'

'On the contrary, sir,' said the Doctor encouragingly. 'I think we can!'

'By use of your magic?' asked Sir Edward hopefully.

'Well—by creating an illusion anyway,' said the Doctor. 'I'll need to fetch a few odds-and-ends from the TARDIS.'

'Your magic will need to be powerful indeed to discourage Irongron.'

'Don't worry, it will!'

'And what do we do?' asked Sarah.

The Doctor smiled. 'My kind of magic takes lots of preparation. There'll be plenty of work for everyone.'

As the morning sunshine streamed through the windows, Irongron was already buckling on his battle-armour.

Bloodaxe, fully armoured and clutching his battle-axe, clanked into the hall. 'The men are ready, Captain.'

'Good.' Irongron tested the edge on his sword and thrust it into his sheath. 'For such an easy conquest as this 'tis scarce worth strapping on armour. You and I alone, good Bloodaxe, could take Sir Edward's castle.'

'Indeed we could, Captain.'

Irongron's mind was leaping ahead to fresh conquests. 'When Sir Edward's castle is mine, I shall use his treasure to hire more soldiers. And with Linx to arm them with his magic weapons—who shall stand against us?'

Linx appeared, his alien features covered by the helmet. From beneath it his voice boomed, 'When does the fighting start?'

Irongron laughed. 'Why, in the time it takes to ride from here to Sir Edward's castle.'

'I shall come with you.'

Irongron stared at him. 'You, Linx? My oath!' He grinned broadly at Bloodaxe. 'Can you see *that* running up a scaling ladder?'

Linx's eyes glowed red at the mockery, but he said evenly, 'I have an interest in seeing the battle.'

Irongron looked curiously at him. 'Those red eyes have a thirst for blood, eh? Then come you shall. Bloodaxe! Find our bold star warrior a horse!'

Yawning after what felt like far too little sleep, Sarah made her way up the winding staircase to the little tower room that the Doctor had taken over for his laboratory. She found the Doctor stirring an evil-smelling powder in an enormous wooden bowl. He was wide-awake and infuriatingly cheerful. Perhaps he didn't need sleep, thought Sarah. She unwrapped her bundle and tipped it out in front of him. It held dozens of little bags made from rough sacking. 'Here you are. I hope it's what you wanted. Lady Eleanor's got every serving wench in the castle sewing away like mad.'

'Told you there'd be plenty of work for everyone, didn't I?' The Doctor picked up one of the bags, opened it, and began filling it with the powder from the bowl. When the bag was full he turned to another in which a number of lengths of twine lay soaking in a clear fluid. Fishing one of the lengths out, the Doctor used it to tie the bag closed at the neck, taking care to leave a dangling length of twine. He picked up another bag and started the whole process all over again.

'Typically masculine arrangement,' said Sarah teasingly. 'The womenfolk do all the hard work and you get all the fun.'

The Doctor sniffed. 'If you think preparing this singularly unpleasant compound is fun, Sarah . . . How's the rest of it going?'

'Pretty well. Sir Edward's painting the faces. He turned out to be quite an artist. Everything'll be ready soon.'

'Excellent,' said the Doctor cheerfully. 'You know, I'm quite glad I decided to stay.'

'*You* decided?'

'I'd have liked a go at the painting myself,' he went on wistfully, 'but I'm not much of a hand with a brush, or a palette knife come to that. Old Rembrandt gave me a few lessons once, but I never really got the hang of it . . .'

'Rembrandt?' said Sarah incredulously. 'You mean you can go anywhere you like in that TARDIS? Any place, any time?'

'Well—within reason. Mind you, the steering still needs one or two minor adjustments.'

'Why are you staying here? Why don't you just clear off to somewhere safer?'

'Because I've got a job to do, Sarah. One that affects the future of all your species.'

'My species? You're talking as if you weren't human.'

The Doctor tied another bag. 'Ah, well, yes. The definition of humanity is a very complex question . . .'

'You know perfectly well what I mean, Doctor. Are you or aren't you?'

'If you mean am I a native of the planet Terra, as you are—no, I'm not.'

'What are you then?'

The Doctor sighed—he hated explanations. 'If you must know, I'm a Time Lord. My people are very keen to stamp out unlicensed time travel. You can think of us as galactic ticket inspectors if you like!'

Sarah yawned. Somehow the Doctor's explanation only made her more confused. 'Galactic ticket inspectors,' she muttered. 'Oh boy. Could I do with a nice cup of tea!' She looked down at the Doctor who was still working busily away. His long fingers moved with nimble speed and soon most of the little bags were filled and tied. 'You're quite serious about all this, aren't you, Doctor?'

'About what I do, yes. But not necessarily about the way I do it. For instance, do you know what's in these bags?'

'No idea.'

The Doctor grinned mischievously. 'Well, you might say this was a special smoking mixture. Saltpetre, sulphur, fat . . . and a few extra ingredients of my own . . .'

There came the sound of a distant horn. The Doctor looked up. 'That'll be Irongron, I imagine. We'd better get a move on. I think battle's about to commence!'

12

The Doctor's Magic

At the head of his little army, Irongron rode out of the
forest, Linx and Bloodaxe close behind him. As the
castle came in view he reined to a halt, raising his hand
as a signal to the column.

Handing the reins to a man-at-arms, Irongron dismounted. He peered ahead of him, shading his eyes
against the sun. Directly in front of him was a short
stretch of rough, open ground. On the other side, the
east wall of Sir Edward's castle, the only one not protected by the moat. Irongron stared hard at the long
turreted wall. At every single embrasure the morning
sunlight glinted on helmet and pike. The wall was lined
with armed men. Irongron gave a howl of rage. 'We
have been tricked, Bloodaxe! That dog of a squire
swore Sir Edward had but a few old men to guard his
castle.'

Bloodaxe came to stand beside his Captain. 'Lord
Salisbury must have sent him help.'

'Edward's messenger to Salisbury lies in our dungeons. Those cannot be Salisbury's men.'

Linx shouldered his way forward. 'Why do you wait?
What will be your first method of attack?'

Irongron turned away in disgust. 'We do not attack.
We return to my castle.'

'You fear to fight?' There was contempt in Linx's
voice. 'We Sontarans say, the greater the odds, the
greater the glory.'

'I fear nothing, toad-face,' snarled Irongron. 'But my men fight for reward—and there is small profit in being butchered for naught.'

Bloodaxe said gloomily. 'We have but few men, Sir Linx, and Sir Edward now holds his walls with too strong a force.'

'Then use the weapons that I made for you. They have the range to slay your enemies on their walls.'

Irongron tugged his beard. 'Aye, the new weapons. By my oath, Linx, when I'm king you shall be my general!'

The Doctor and Sarah crouched down behind a soldier —not a real soldier, but a painted figure of wood and canvas. Only the steel helmet above the painted face was real, and the pike lashed to its side. Similar dummy figures filled the embrasures along the length of the wall. Hal the archer and the few real men-at-arms were hiding at intervals along the wall.

Sarah grinned at the sight of the furiously arguing figures below them. 'That's made them stop and think, anyway.'

The Doctor pointed to a squat armoured figure next to Irongron. 'I thought Linx wouldn't be able to resist coming along . . . Sontarans can't resist a war. I'm afraid he won't be so easy to fool as old Irongron.'

'This must be very minor league stuff to him, surely?'

The Doctor shrugged. 'He's like a little boy, stirring up the red ants and the black ants for sport—just something to stop him getting bored.'

There was a good deal of confusion and milling about amongst the attackers below. Weapons were being unloaded from a cart, passed out amongst the men. Irongron's troops formed themselves into an uneven line and began advancing on the castle. They raised the weapons to their shoulders. The Doctor put his hand on Sarah's head and shoved her below the embrasure. 'Keep down!'

There was a ragged volley from below. Heavy bullets whizzed past their heads, some of them chipping chunks of stone from the battlements. Holes appeared in the canvas body of the dummy. 'They've got guns!' said Sarah indignantly. The Doctor nodded.

'We can thank our Sontaran friend for that!'

Irongron shaded his eyes again, and glared along the battlements. There was a mailed figure at every embrasure, just as before. Some of his men might have missed—but not all of them . . .

Bloodaxe confirmed his thoughts. 'Not a man of the enemy has fallen, Captain.'

Irongron turned angrily to Linx. 'Your weapons do not work, star warrior.'

'Your men do not shoot straight!' Linx snatched a rifle from the nearest man-at-arms; re-loaded and threw it to his shoulder. Moving forward he fired at the figure directly above him. There was the crack of the shot, and black smoke from the gun.

'You missed, star warrior,' jeered Irongron.

Linx tossed the weapon back to the man-at-arms.

'I never miss. Those soldiers do not move or fall. They are not living men.'

Irongron looked at the motionless figures lining the battlements. 'Dummies! I smell that fox the Doctor behind this!' He turned and shouted to his men. 'They are but dummies, lads. Men of straw. Bring up the scaling ladders—we attack!'

Crouching down low, the Doctor dragged a heavy wooden tub out of the corner turret and along to the centre of the battlements. Sarah came behind him, carefully shielding a smoking lamp. She put it down beside the tub and looked up at the Doctor. 'Now what?'

'We'll just let them get a bit closer.'

Staggering under the weight of the long, unwieldy scaling ladders, Irongron's men lurched forward. Unopposed they reached the castle walls and began swaying the ladders into place.

The Doctor's tub was filled with the round powder-filled bags. They looked rather like little Christmas puddings. The Doctor took one of the bags from the tub, and held the end of its twine in the flame of the lamp. The saltpetre-soaked twine caught fire at once, sputtering fiercely.

Almost carelessly, the Doctor tossed the bag over the battlements. He reached for another . . .

The man-at-arms steadied the base of the scaling ladder so that his fellows could begin to climb. Suddenly, a little fizzing bag plopped down at his feet. He bent to pick it up—and jumped back with a yell of fear as the bag exploded.

Other bags were falling amongst the attackers. They exploded one by one, sending out clouds of dense orange smoke, which hung about the base of the walls like a bank of fog, smothering Irongron's men. From this orange fog came bangs, flashes, showers of dazzling sparks and weird howling sounds. The attacking soldiers milled about in confusion.

This was an age in which explosives in any form were still unknown. Bangs and flashes and clouds of stinking smoke could have only one explanation. 'Devil's work,' screamed one of the soldiers. 'They have raised the fires of hell against us!' The panic spread like a plague, and the terrified attackers turned and fled. As they ran, arrows whizzed down from the battlements to speed them on their way.

At the edge of the woods, Irongron paused and tried to rally his men, but it was hopeless. Coughing and choking, eyes wide with terror, they stampeded past him. Irongron shook his fist at the castle—and an arrow thudded into the tree trunk, inches from his head. He turned and ran for his horse, shouting, 'Away, lads! This is devil's work right enough!' Irongron could have saved his breath. Most of his men were already well ahead of him.

A moment later, only Linx was left on the field of battle. He looked longingly at the castle for a moment. Then, mounting his terrified horse, he rode off after the others.

High on the battlements Sarah was doing a celebratory war dance. She hugged the Doctor and slapped him on the back. The Doctor smiled. 'I share your jubilation, Sarah—but I think we'd better get back inside before the smoke rises. It'll hang about the walls for some time, I'm afraid.'

'What is it, Doctor? Some kind of poison gas?'

The Doctor was shocked. 'Good heavens no. What do you take me for? Just an assortment of bad smells with a few bangs and flashes thrown in for good measure. A sort of combination stink-bomb and firework!'

A whiff of orange smoke drifted over the battlements. Sarah gasped and held her nose. 'You're sure it's not poison gas?' The Doctor grinned. 'Totally harmless, I assure you. Come on, let's get back inside.'

Irongron staggered into his great hall, tearing off his

armour and hurling it to one side. 'Wine!' he roared. 'Bring me wine, I say. Wine to clear the dust from my throat and the stench from my nostrils!'

Meg the serving wench hurried up with a brimming flagon. Irongron drained it at a gulp. 'More, wench, more! Am I a sparrow to quench my thirst with a few scant drops?' Meg brought forward the wine jug and refilled his flagon. Irongron swigged deeply, and looked disgustedly around him. His men-at-arms were straggling sheepishly into the hall. Never a particularly smart body of men, they were grimy, ragged and exhausted by their panic-stricken retreat through the forest. As Irongron's scornful gaze swept over them they looked away, ashamed to meet his eye. There was a moment's awful silence. Then, 'Mice!' bellowed Irongron. 'A few loud noises, a few bad smells and you scatter like sheep!'

Only Bloodaxe dared to answer. 'It was devil's work, Captain, black sorcery. You said as much yourself. This wizard they call the Doctor has joined Sir Edward. He threw all the fires and stenches of hell at us.'

Contemptuously Irongron surveyed his crestfallen band. 'With poltroons like these, it were ill work to lay siege to a hen-coop.'

Bloodaxe did his best to defend his mates. 'They do but need food and rest, Captain, time to recover their bold spirits.'

The bedraggled robbers cheered up a little. But not for long. Irongron rose and glared at them, biting out his words with savage emphasis. 'At dawn tomorrow we attack again. This time we take Sir Edward's castle, or I will see that every last man of you perishes in the attempt.' He paused impressively. 'Chicken-hearted knaves,' he roared. 'Begone from my sight!'

Thankfully Irongron's men fled from the hall. As they left, a squat figure shouldered its way through them.

'Did I not see you leading their retreat—*Captain*?' There was a wealth of scorn in the last word.

Irongron leaped to his feet and towered menacingly over the Sontaran. 'Taunt me not, you insolent little toad.' He lugged out his sword. 'Or by heaven I'll see if the colour of your blood is red like mortal man's.'

Unimpressed, Linx looked up at the furious robber chief. 'You earth creatures give up too easily. I doubt if you have the potential to make a truly successful military species.'

'And you, Linx? You claim to like war yet I have not seen you do many deeds of valour this day!'

'I came only to observe. I should have known better than to look for interest in the struggles of primitives.'

Choking with rage, Irongron brandished his sword over Linx's head. 'I warn you, toad-face . . .'

Linx turned away. 'Threaten me once more,' he said casually, 'and I shall destroy you.'

Goaded beyond endurance, Irongron raised his sword and Linx's arm swept out and swatted him almost carelessly away. The result was extraordinary. Irongron's massive figure flew backwards across the hall, went head over heels across the banqueting table, smashed into the wall beyond and slid slowly to the ground.

Ignoring the horrified Bloodaxe, Linx strode across and looked down at his victim. After a moment Irongron opened his eyes and stared unbelievingly at him.

'Primitives,' said Linx coldly. 'Childish, stupid, squabbling primitives. It is fortunate that my time amongst you is almost over.' He turned away and marched out.

Bloodaxe rushed to help his Captain rise. Irongron got slowly to his feet. As the meaning of the Sontaran's last remark sunk into his half-stunned brain his expression changed all at once from rage to cunning.

The atmosphere was very different at Sir Edward's castle; they were having a victory feast. Lady Eleanor looked fondly at her husband, thinking it was years since she had seen him in such good spirits.

'More wine for the Doctor,' ordered Sir Edward, and a maid-servant hurried forward with a jug.

'No, no, I couldn't possibly,' protested the Doctor. 'Oh well, if you insist. Perhaps just a small one.' He caught Sarah's eye and grinned.

'Those knaves ran like rabbits,' said Sir Edward exultantly. 'The finest sight that ever I saw, Doctor, and all thanks to you and your wizardry.'

'Oh, we all did our part, Sir Edward,' said the Doctor modestly.

'And now, with your magic to protect us, our troubles are over.'

'Not quite, I'm afraid. Irongron's pride has been hurt. He's lost face before his men.'

Sarah swallowed a mouthful of chicken. 'The Doctor thinks Irongron will attack again.'

'Then you shall affright the knaves with more of your sorceries, Doctor!' said Sir Edward jubilantly.

The Doctor's face was grave. 'That won't work indefinitely, I'm afraid. We had the advantage of total surprise this time. It won't be so easy to scare them off again.'

The happiness faded from Sir Edward's face. 'Then we have gained no more than a brief respite?'

'Not necessarily. I do have another idea.'

Sir Edward brightened. 'Then let us hear it, Doctor. So far, your counsel has served us well.'

The Doctor paused, gathering the attention of his

audience. 'There is only one sure way to prevent Iron-gron from capturing your castle, Sir Edward.'

'And that is?'

'You must capture his!'

13

Counter Attack

The Doctor's simple announcement caused utter consternation.

'You advise the impossible, Doctor,' said Sir Edward in dismay.

'Not necessarily.' The Doctor produced a sheet of parchment and handed it to Lady Eleanor. 'My lady, are you familiar with these herbs?'

'Ragwort, henbane, night-shade, love-in-a-mist . . .' Rapidly she ran her eye over the rest of the list. 'Most we have in the castle kitchens, the rest grow in the woods nearby.'

'Excellent. I want to brew up a little draught, you see.'

Lady Eleanor's eyes gleamed. 'You will mix a potion and poison the dog?'

'No, no,' said the Doctor hurriedly. 'Just something to calm him down a little. A kind of tranquilliser . . .'

Irongron drained his wine, and glared round the hall in half-drunken fury. 'I should have slain the filthy toad, there and then. I should have carved him into collops on the spot!'

Bloodaxe stared blearily at his Captain. 'Aye, Master. It puzzles me to know why you did not!'

Irongron shot him a suspicious glare, looking for any hint of sarcasm. But there was only honest puzzlement on Bloodaxe's long face. Satisfied, Irongron leaned forward and whispered, 'Aye, well, 'twas a question of high policy, do you see? Above your understanding, good Bloodaxe.'

Bloodaxe looked enquiringly at him, and Irongron went on, 'As yet we still need Linx's aid. Weapons he has promised me, and by the stars, weapons I shall have. Wonderful, magical weapons to crumble the castles of those who oppose me into dust. When those weapons are mine, then, and only then, shall Linx die by my hand.'

'A cunning plan, Captain,' said Bloodaxe with drunken solemnity.

Irongron gave a self-satisfied nod. 'Aye, 'tis well for you dolts you have me to guide you. There's more to war than hard strokes, my good Bloodaxe.'

Bloodaxe nodded, his faith in his Captain restored. 'Aye, Captain. Yours is indeed a towering intelligence!'

While Irongron brooded over his revenge, the sentries at the main gate were watching in some astonishment as two strange figures came trudging towards them. They wore the brown robes and hoods of wandering friars. One was tall and thin, with robes that were much too short, the other smaller and slighter, in robes that seemed far too long.

As the strange-looking friars attempted to enter the castle, two pikes came down to bar their way. 'Hold, friar,' growled the older of the two pikemen. 'What business have you here?'

The tall friar spoke in a solemn voice. 'We come to beg alms of the good Captain Irongron. The fame of his charity has spread far and wide!'

The sentry's jaw dropped in astonishment. He was about to chase them away, when he had a sudden inspiration. Winking at his companion he stepped back, and bowed elaborately. 'Pass, Holy Father! You will find Captain Irongron in the great hall. He is indeed a most kindly and charitable man, renowned for the sweetness of his temper.'

'Heaven will reward you, my son,' said the tall friar solemnly. He and his companion crossed the courtyard and entered the castle.

As soon as they were out of sight the sentries collapsed with laughter, hugging themselves in their mirth. The older one jabbed his companion in the ribs. 'Let us hope the good friars are fleet of foot—or there will soon be two new martyrs in heaven!'

Once inside, the two friars turned away from the great hall, and went down a narrow corridor that led towards the rear of the castle. The Doctor looked down at Sarah and grinned. 'I knew they'd never be able to resist it!'

They stripped off their friar's robes and stuffed them behind a wall-tapestry. The Doctor wore his usual clothes, but Sarah was now dressed as a serving maid.

'Come on Sarah,' said the Doctor. 'Let's take a look at Irongron's workshop.'

Huddled in their borrowed cloaks, two wandering friars trudged back towards their monastery in some confusion. They were grateful for Sir Edward's handsome donation . . . but what was the Abbot going to say about their missing robes . . .

The Doctor led the way down the steps, into Linx's workshop. Sarah looked in astonishment at the computer, the grey-faced men toiling at the benches and the gleaming metal sphere that took up the far corner. 'What is that thing, Doctor?'

'A Sontaran scout ship. Small, but tremendously

powerful—just like its owner!'

Sarah looked at the silent, grey-faced workers. 'Why don't they take any notice of us?'

'Deep hypnosis,' said the Doctor briefly. One of the scientists detached himself from the rest and came shuffling towards them.

'Ah, there you are, Doctor. Back again eh?'

Sarah looked at him in amazement. 'Professor Rubeish!'

The old man produced what looked like a pair of spectacles on a stick. He peered at Sarah through this home-made lorgnette. 'Oh, it's you, young lady. I told you she was involved, Doctor. We should have reported her as I suggested.'

The Doctor smiled at Sarah. 'I'm very glad we didn't.' He looked quickly round the workshop. The benches were far less cluttered now. Most of the damaged equipment had already been repaired and replaced in the scout ship. 'A few more hours and that ship will be ready for blast-off.'

Rubeish nodded. 'He's been working these people at a killing pace. Come over here.' He led them to a corner of the workshop, where exhausted men lay piled in a heap. Their tasks completed, many of the scientists had collapsed into a semi-coma. 'No sleep, precious little food,' said Rubeish bitterly. 'They've been dropping like flies.'

Sarah looked at the pile of human bodies in horror. Most of the men seemed just barely alive. 'We've got to help them, Doctor.'

'I'm afraid there's no time, Sarah,' said the Doctor sadly.

'But some of them will die if they don't get attention soon.'

'They'll all die if we don't stop Linx, and so will we.

When that ship blasts off there'll be a tremendous explosion. Everyone in this castle will die!' The Doctor knelt beside one of the unconscious men and peered closely into his eyes . . .

Half-tired, half-drunk, Irongron and Bloodaxe dozed at the table in the great hall, heads buried in their arms. A sudden shattering crash jerked them awake. They jumped up in alarm to see Linx standing before them. An enormous wooden crate lay at his feet—they had been woken by the noise when Linx had thrown it down. 'I keep my bargain, Irongron. These are the rest of the weapons I promised you.'

Irongron tried to drag the crate towards him, and found he could barely move it. He lifted the lid and took out one of the rifles. 'More weapons from the stars! My thanks, good toad-face—good Linx, I mean. And what of the new iron man you promised me?'

'I shall complete the improved fighting robot before I leave—if I have time.'

Irongron's face hardened. 'If you wish to leave at all, good Linx, you'd do well to learn to obey me. I say you will not go yet.'

'Do you dare to threaten me? I shall leave when I am ready—and that will be very soon.'

'Will you carry your starship on your back, good toad? You needed my knaves to bring it here and you need them to take it hence.'

'The ship is repaired now. Evidently you have no understanding of the forces used in interstellar travel. I repeat, I leave when I am ready. You would be foolish to attempt to stop me.'

Unaware that Linx was already on his way back, the Doctor was shining a torch-like device into the eyes of one of the hypnotised scientists.

'What are you doing?' asked Rubeish peevishly.

'Trying to break the hypnosis. It's very deep but if the brain receives signals, it might work . . .'

'Even if it does, I still can't see what you intend . . .'

'Don't you want to get back to the twentieth century?'

'Steak!' said Rubeish wistfully. 'Mushrooms, lobster, chocolate. Oh, dear me yes, Doctor. It's very interesting here, but I'm not as pure a scientist as I thought!'

The Doctor continued his examination. 'If I can get these poor fellows to respond, I can use Linx's osmic projector to return them to their own time.'

Sarah stared at him. 'Osmic projector?'

'Back there, on the table.' The Doctor pointed to a large and complicated-looking piece of alien equipment which stood a little apart from the rest. It looked something like a futuristic film projector.

'Why not just send 'em back as they are?' asked Sarah practically.

'Too risky. With their minds in this state, the temporal transition could damage them permanently. No use sending back mindless idiots.'

'Never heard so much gobbledygook in my life,' muttered Rubeish. 'Still, I expect you know what you're talking about.'

'Polka time!' said the Doctor exultantly.

'What?'

'I've found the anti-hypnotic beat—it's like polka time. Look, he's responding.'

Rubeish looked. The scientist was muttering and stirring, like someone roused from a very deep sleep. He moaned and tried to sit up—just as heavy footsteps approached the workshop door. The Doctor grabbed

Sarah and dragged her behind a column.

Linx came down the stairs into the workshop. He paused, staring around him suspiciously as if sensing something wrong. He looked at the huddled bodies in the corner. One of the discarded slave-workers was moaning, trying weakly to get to his feet.

Linx frowned. He walked over to those few slaves still at work, and watched them for a moment. One of them staggered wearily back and collapsed. Linx snatched the ray-gun from his belt and gave the fallen scientist a low-intensity blast. The man moaned and twitched, but he was still too feeble to rise. 'Up!' commanded Linx. 'Get up and work or I will kill you!' He gave the writhing body another blast.

The Doctor felt Sarah struggling to rise. He pushed her back out of sight, then stepped out of hiding and confronted Linx. 'Leave the man alone.'

Immediately the ray-gun was raised to cover him. 'Aaah!' Linx gave a growling purr of satisfaction. 'How fortunate that you have returned, Doctor. My failure to destroy you was the one thing that marred the pleasure of my departure from this miserable planet!'

'Don't you want to know *why* I returned, Linx?'

Linx raised the ray-gun. 'No. It is of no interest to me.'

'Wait!' The Doctor was talking for his life. 'I came to offer you my help.'

Intrigued, Linx paused. 'We are sworn enemies, Doctor. Why should you help me?'

'We've more in common than you think. You want to leave Earth, don't you? Well, I want you to go, provided you undo the harm you've caused. De-hypnotise these men, and send them home. Help me capture Irongron and turn him over to Sir Edward. Recover all the weapons you've made and stack them up in this room.

115

I'll help you to complete the repairs to your scout ship and you can take off. The blast will destroy weapons and castle together and you can get back to your precious war.'

Linx listened to this speech in impassive silence. When the Doctor finished, he still said nothing.

'Well?' said the Doctor impatiently. 'What do you say, Commander Linx?'

The wide, lipless mouth stretched in a smile. 'You wish for my answer, Doctor?'

'Yes, of course I do.'

'Then here it is.' Linx set his ray-gun to maximum and fired.

14

The Robot's Return

For a second the Doctor twisted in the deadly red glow. Sarah leaped from hiding and tried to push Linx's arm aside. She was unable to move it more than a fraction, but it was enough to deflect the ray from the Doctor. He collapsed gasping against a pillar.

Linx sent Sarah staggering with a sweep of his arm. 'The female too. It seems I am doubly fortunate.'

Another slave worker staggered and fell. Linx kicked him to his feet. 'Up! Get back to your work!' Groaning the prisoner obeyed.

'Your prisoners are physically exhausted,' said the Doctor painfully. 'They've gone for days without rest.'

'They can still work,' said Linx brutally.

'Not for much longer.'

'I do not need them for much longer. I owe these primitives nothing. My concern is to rejoin the glorious struggle for the supremacy we Sontarans deserve.'

'That's an old familiar tune, Linx. There's no such thing as a super-race.'

'Your Time Lord philosophy is egalitarian twaddle. It is your weak spot.'

The Doctor had almost recovered by now. Luckily his exposure to Linx's ray-gun had been brief. He straightened up, raising his voice. 'Ah, but every species has its weak spot, Linx. For instance, you Sontarans can only be harmed by an attack on the probic vent—the aperture on the back of your neck, where you plug in for your energy.'

From where she stood, Sarah could see a small circular hole at the back of Linx's space-suit—where the nape of the neck would have been on a human being. She wondered why the Doctor was telling Linx something he already knew. Then she realised. The Doctor wasn't telling Linx at all. He was telling Rubeish. The old man had armed himself with a metal bar, and he was creeping slowly up behind the Sontaran. With aggravating slowness Rubeish took out his home-made spectacles and peered through them, assuring himself of his target.

Linx was answering the Doctor. 'In our case, that weakness is a strength, since it ensures that we must always face our enemies. Now, Doctor, to return to the question of your destruction. I imagine it would cause maximum distress if you first witnessed the death of your female companion.' He swung the ray gun on Sarah and she backed away. Linx paused, savouring the moment.

The Doctor gathered his returning strength for a desperate attack—and Rubeish stepped up behind the Sontaran and swung his iron bar, slamming it down on the probic vent. Linx gave a weird howl of agony, and crashed to the ground with a thud that shook the workshop.

'Well done, old chap,' said the Doctor.

Sarah ran across to him. 'Are you all right?'

'Oh, I think so. I only got a brief blast. But I wouldn't have been in a few seconds. Thank you, Sarah.'

'My pleasure,' said Sarah cheerfully. 'Now hadn't we better be getting on with the rest of your master plan?'

'Quite right. You'll be careful, won't you?'

Sarah nodded. 'You too, Doctor.' She hurried up the steps.

The Doctor turned to Rubeish. 'Now, if we can secure our Sontaran friend, Professor, we can get on with restoring his unfortunate victims.'

Rubeish hurried over to a bench and produced a coil of metal-cored plastic flex. 'Will this help?'

The Doctor patted him on the back. 'Rubeish, my dear fellow, you really are invaluable!'

Dragging Linx to one side, they trussed him up with the flex, winding coil after coil around the stocky body.

The Doctor tied a final knot and straightened up. 'There, that should hold him for a time, even on Earth.'

'What do you mean—even on Earth?'

'He comes from a high-gravity planet. Fortunately his muscles are designed for load-bearing, rather than leverage.'

'Fascinating,' said Rubeish. 'You know, Doctor, I'd always assumed that creatures from such a planet would have developed a pressure-balanced physiology. Consider certain types of sea weed . . .'

A voice from the top of the stairs interrupted him. 'Linx! Linx, I say!'

The Doctor dragged Rubeish behind a pillar.

'Linx,' called the voice again.

The Doctor cupped his hands to his mouth and gave a fair imitation of the Sontaran's booming voice. 'Who speaks?'

'Bloodaxe. I come with a message from Captain Irongron. He commands your presence.'

'I am busy,' boomed the Doctor.

'He says you must come soon—or he will send men to fetch you.'

'Too scared to come right in—luckily for us,' muttered the Doctor.

'Who's this Irongron he mentioned?'

'The owner of this castle.'

'Good chap, is he?'

The Doctor smiled. 'Well I wouldn't exactly recommend him for the Royal Society. Now then, Rubeish, you saw how I brought these people round?'

'Yes, yes, a simple repetitive optical stimulus.'

The Doctor passed him the little torch. 'Quite so! I'll leave you to get on with it.'

'And what do you propose to do?'

'I shall re-set this osmic projector and send them back to their own time.'

There came another yell from the top of the stairs. 'Linx, Captain Irongron awaits you! Will you come, or must we drag you forth?'

The Doctor cupped his hands. 'Tell Irongron I am coming,' he boomed. He turned to Rubeish. 'I'm afraid I'll have to find some way of delaying Irongron. We can't have him coming down here.' He looked hurriedly round the workshop. A suit of black armour was standing against the wall. There were a few odds and ends of robotic circuitry scattered about nearby.

The Doctor grinned. 'The Robot! That'll keep him quiet for a while!'

Sarah crept cautiously into the castle kitchens and looked around. There were wine barrels lining the walls, rough wooden tables covered with scraps of food— and a great open fire over which hung an enormous cauldron. Sarah's hand went to the stone bottle in the pocket of her dress . . . and something sharp, cold and metallic touched her throat. She jumped back. A big tough-looking serving-woman was holding a meat skewer to her throat. 'Thief!' hissed the woman angrily.

Sarah drew herself up, and tried to imitate Lady Eleanor's haughty tones. 'Stand aside, scullion. How dare you obstruct me? I'll have you flogged!'

The woman lunged forward, and grabbed her

arm. 'Oh, a fine lady, are you? A lady dressed up as a serving wench.'

Sarah looked down at her plain gown and realised it had been a mistake to try and carry things off with a high hand. She changed her tactics. 'Please,' she whined. 'I'm hungry. The men on the gate let me through, they said you'd give me food. I've tasted neither bread nor meat for nearly a month!'

Meg shifted her grip to Sarah's wrist and twisted her hand, examining the smooth uncalloused palm. 'No, nor done no honest work for longer by the look of you. All right, my girl.' She shoved Sarah towards a table. 'There's a sack of potatoes, and there's a knife . . . I'll give you bread and cheese—but you'll have to earn it!'

Irongron looked up in amazement as a fully-armoured knight stalked into his hall, sword in hand. 'By my oath, what's this then?'

The knight spoke in a deep hollow voice. 'I am a gift to Captain Irongron, from the one who made me, my master Commander Linx.' Stiffly the figure brandished its sword.

Irongron got slowly to his feet and walked round the black-armoured figure. 'Another iron warrior, Bloodaxe . . . though different in shape. Linx promised me a second.' He peered at the closed visor. 'Why did not Linx obey my summons himself?'

'My master toils to make more fighting robots. He sent me as proof of this. Now I must return to him.' He made for the door.

'Hold,' roared Irongron. 'I would see something of the metal of this gift. Can you fight, iron man?'

'That is my purpose.'

'Then fight me!' Drawing his sword, Irongron advanced to the attack.

Inside the suit of armour the Doctor sighed. He had hoped that his mere appearance in the robot disguise would keep Irongron quiet for a while. He hadn't expected to provide a practical demonstration.

'I am made to fight for you, not against you,' he boomed. 'There will be damage to my circuits. I must return to the workroom.'

Irongron leaped in front of him. 'Cease thy gabble, iron man, and fight!'

He swung a savage blow at the Doctor's head. The Doctor parried it, and Irongron struck again, and again . . .

The hall was filled with the clangour of sword play as Irongron rained blow after blow upon the black knight. The Doctor concentrated simply on defending himself, fending off Irongron's wild swings with comparative ease, since, luckily, Irongron's swordsmanship relied more on brute force than skill.

At last Irongron lowered his sword and stepped back gasping. 'Stop!'

Bloodaxe was popeyed with astonishment. 'This iron man is indeed a marvel, Captain. Never have I seen a finer swordsman!'

Irongron mopped his forehead with his sleeve. 'Come, join me, Bloodaxe. 'Tis fine sport this. We'll try the thing's strength to the utmost.'

Bloodaxe drew his sword and advanced to join his Captain. Inside the suit of armour the Doctor groaned again, and raised his sword . . .

Sarah threw another potato into the stewpot. From outside the kitchen came shouts and yells, and the clash of steel. She looked up, worried. 'What's all the noise?'

Meg grunted. 'They are fighting again in the great hall, I'll warrant. Men are like children, ever fond of noise and brawling. Get on with your work, girl.'

She stood determinedly over Sarah, watching her suspiciously. Sarah sighed, and picked up another potato.

By now a crowd had gathered. Drawn by the rumour of Linx's latest marvel, the men-at-arms flocked to see this incredible iron knight, who could hold two swordsmen in play at the same time.

The black knight fought like a demon. Whirling, stamping, slashing, it parried every blow. Not once did either of the two opponents break through its guard.

For a second time Irongron stepped back. 'Hold! Hold, I say!' He looked across at his gasping lieutenant. 'We must slow this iron man's speed a little.' He turned to a bowman watching by the door. 'Stick me a few bolts through this creature. We'll see if it fights as well with an arrow in its gizzard. Aye, and if that fails, we'll lop off its head like the first, and try it then!'

The man-at-arms raised his crossbow and took aim.

15

Shooting Gallery

Enough was enough, decided the Doctor. In his normal voice he said, 'Don't you think that's a bit unsporting, old chap, shooting a sitting bird?'

Irongron gaped at him. 'This creature speaks like some Norman ninny. Lift your visor, sir knight!'

'I cannot reveal my face to you, Irongron,' said the Doctor solemnly.

'And why not?'

'It might cause you to have a seizure!'

Irongron came slowly forward. He reached out and lifted the black knight's visor. At the sight of the Doctor's face he jumped back with a yell of alarm. 'The wizard!'

'I did warn you,' said the Doctor apologetically—and made a dash for the door.

'Seize him,' yelled Irongron. The Doctor disappeared beneath a pile of men-at-arms. Subdued by sheer weight of numbers, he was hauled from beneath the pile and forced to his knees before Irongron.

Irongron looked thoughtfully at the Doctor's neck, and raised his sword . . . Then he paused. 'No! The sword is too quick and clean a death for such as you, Doctor. Since you are a wizard—by wizardry you shall die!'

As Sarah peeled the last of the potatoes, a depressed-looking serving wench appeared. She was promptly seized by Meg and set to work, mixing a huge pot of oatmeal. Sarah listened for more sounds from the great hall. Everything was quiet now, but somehow the silence was more sinister than the noise. Meg cuffed the serving wench. 'Go easy with that oatmeal, girl. It's only pikemen we're feeding, not horses!' She turned on Sarah. 'And keep an eye on that stew. If you burn Captain Irongron's supper he'll cut your liver out!'

Sarah tossed in the last few potatoes and stirred the bubbling pot with a long wooden ladle. 'Is this all for Irongron?'

'Him and his special cronies, his chamber guard.'

'What about the sentries on the gate? Don't they get stew?'

Meg was shocked. 'What? Meat for common soldiers? They get oatmeal, and lucky to get it. And lusty enough they are on that. You watch yourself when you take out the pot!'

Sarah gave the stewpot another stir. 'I'm not afraid of men, they don't own the world. Why should we always have to cook and carry for them?'

Meg looked baffled. 'Why, what else should we do?'

'Stand up for ourselves, stop being treated like slaves.'

The little serving girl said wonderingly, 'But we *are* slaves.'

'Then free yourselves. Don't you want to be free?'

Meg began filling a huge jug from one of the wine barrels. 'Women will never be free while there are men in the world. We have our place.'

'Subservient poppycock,' said Sarah indignantly. 'You're still living in the middle ages.' Sarah shut up, remembering these poor women were doing exactly that.

Meg picked up the jug of wine. 'Foolish thoughts, my girl. Keep them to yourself, or you'll not live long enough to grow wise. I must take them their wine.' She stumped off.

The little servant girl edged away from Sarah, obviously thinking her mad. Turning her back to the girl, Sarah slipped the stone bottle from her pocket and poured a good half of the murky-looking fluid it contained into the stewpot. Concealing the bottle in her dress, she edged closer to the serving girl, who was still stirring her oatmeal.

Sarah gave a cry of alarm. 'Look at that great spider!'

The girl screamed and jumped back. Sarah got between her and the pot, and poured the rest of the Doctor's potion into the oatmeal. She smiled reassuringly at the girl and said, 'It's all right, it's gone now.' The girl picked up her ladle and went on stirring.

Professor Rubeish was de-hypnotising the last of Linx's slave-workers, humming softly to remind himself of the correct polka rhythm. 'Oh see me dance the polka, tra-lal-lal-lal-lal-la.' The scientist shook his head and stared dazedly about him. Rubeish helped him to his feet and pushed him gently over to the others. He surveyed the little group of dazed, enfeebled men. 'Now listen, all of you. You've been kidnapped and hypnotised, but you're all about to be rescued—I hope. There's a machine here that will send you home. Unfortunately I don't know how to work it. The chap who does has vanished but I expect he'll pop up again soon, he usually does . . . Until then you must all carry on as if you were still hypnotised.'

There was a confused babble of questions, but Rubeish held up his hand. 'Don't start asking a lot of silly questions, I don't know the answers any more than you do. Now quiet, all of you, someone's coming.'

*

As the scientists obediently slumped down, Irongron appeared at the top of the steps yelling, 'Linx! Where are you? I have news . . .'

When there was no reply, he came down into the workshop. 'Linx? Linx, you dog, where are you hiding?' Irongron hunted round, until at last he found the Sontaran lying bound and unconscious in a dark corner of the workshop. Irongron laughed, and prodded him with his toe. 'By the sword, so there you are, you dragon-eyed toad!' Linx's eyes flickered open, and his face twisted with rage as he realised his position. He began struggling furiously.

Irongron drew his sword. He looked thoughtfully at the helpless Sontaran for a moment, then decided he still needed him. He sawed through the plastic flex with his sword. 'Who put these bonds on you?'

'The Doctor,' croaked Linx. 'I was struck down from behind.'

Irongron laughed. 'That's rich. I came to tell you that the Doctor has been captured.'

The Sontaran struggled to his feet. 'Where is he?'

'About to die,' said Irongron cheerfully. 'Come with me, Linx. You shall see rare sport!'

Stripped of his armour, the Doctor stood against the rear wall of the great hall. Pikemen stood at the corners to his left and to his right, though they kept well clear of him. By the main door at the other end of the hall stood half-a-dozen of Irongron's men, all armed with the new rifles.

Irongron, Linx, Bloodaxe and a scattering of men-at-arms stood just behind the riflemen. Meg came round with a jug, and poured wine for them.

'May I enquire the purpose of all this tomfoolery?' asked the Doctor acidly.

Irongron smiled evilly. 'I would not have your death be in vain, good sorcerer. I intend it shall be of use to me.'

'I will do nothing that will help you, Irongron.'

Irongron rubbed his hands together. 'Nay, but you are wrong. My men lack practice with the new weapons. A living target will better their aim before tomorrow's battle.' He tapped the nearest rifleman on the shoulder. 'You, fellow, shoot!' Startled, the man fired. The Doctor ducked, and a chip of stone flew from the wall, a good foot away from his head. Irongron laughed. 'The knave shoots so ill, you were safer to stand still, Doctor.' He tapped the next man. 'Shoot!' The next man fired. He missed—though only by inches.

'See,' called Irongron, 'the aim improves. Be patient, Doctor, we shall hit the target in good time.'

'I'm in no great hurry, I assure you,' called the Doctor.

Irongron rocked with laughter. 'By the stars, I grow almost fond of this wizard.' His voice hardened. 'Shoot when you will, lads—a bag of gold to the man who brings him down!'

Sarah looked up as Meg came back into the hall. 'What's happening now? I can hear shooting.'

'More tomfoolery,' grunted Meg. 'They have captured this wizard they call the Doctor. They are slaying him now in the great hall with these new devil's weapons. Though what's wrong with a good old-fashioned axe . . .'

Sarah pushed past her and disappeared down the corridor.

Coolly the Doctor calculated his chances. Surely his luck must run out before very long. His only advantage

128

was that the men-at-arms were still uneasy with their new weapons. But they were improving all the time. Some of the more recent shots had missed only by inches. The Doctor watched a rifleman take careful aim, waited till the last possible moment, and then threw himself to the ground. As the rifle cracked he rolled over, and leaped to his feet, moving constantly to and fro in a random pattern.

'By the stars,' said Irongron delightedly. 'The fellow hops about like a flea on a griddle!'

Linx was impatient for the Doctor's death. 'Give me a weapon and I will destroy him.'

Irongron shook his head. 'What, and spoil good sport, old toad?'

The Doctor threw himself to one side as another man fired. 'Never fear, Linx, my knaves will soon bring him down. See, the fellow tires . . .'

Sarah paused when she came in sight of the door to the great hall . . . It was crowded with men-at-arms—no chance to rescue the Doctor here. She turned and ran up a narrow flight of stairs. They led her up into the tiny minstrels' gallery that overlooked the great hall. From this vantage point, Sarah took in the scene below in one horrified glance. The Doctor dodging to and fro, the line of riflemen at the other end of the hall, Linx and Irongron and the rest of them watching . . .

A rifle cracked and stone chips flew from the wall, very close to the Doctor's head.

Sarah looked round desperately. There must be a way, she thought. There must. Then she saw the chandelier.

It hung suspended by chains from the centre of the hall, a huge iron ring with holders for hundreds of candles. No doubt in happier days it had been used to light the hall for important feasts. In order that the candles could be re-lit, and replaced when necessary, a rope was attached to the chandelier so that it could be pulled across to the minstrels' gallery and the candles lit from there. That was its position now, the heavy iron ring resting on the edge of the gallery. It was like a kind of trapeze, thought Sarah—and the plan seemed to leap into her mind. It was as simple as it was dangerous —but if the Doctor reacted quickly enough, it would offer him one slender chance.

Sarah ran to the edge of the gallery, untied the rope holding back the chandelier. She yelled, 'Doctor! Up here!' and gave the thing a mighty shove, sending it swinging pendulum-like above the hall.

The Doctor looked up and saw the chandelier beginning its swing. He dashed forward, leaped on to the table, sprang high in the air and caught the iron ring as it swung overhead. High in the air he flew, over the heads of the astonished riflemen, over Linx and Irongron and the others. Letting go at the end of the swing, he shot straight through the open door. He landed in the corridor, rolled over, sprang to his feet, ran to the door of the hall and slammed it in Irongron's astonished face, dropping the locking-bar into place. He turned and saw Sarah running down the stairs towards him.

The Doctor grinned. 'Just like the daring young man on the flying trapeze, eh? Thank you again, Miss Smith!'

The hall door was shaking under angry blows and they heard Irongron's voice. 'After them! Kill them both!'

'I think it's time we left,' said the Doctor solemnly, and they ran down the hall and out into the yard. As they sprinted towards the drawbridge they heard the door burst open behind them. There were fierce, angry yells and the sound of pursuing feet.

Alerted by the noise, the guards at the gate stepped forward to bar their way. Now they had enemies both in front and behind them, thought Sarah despairingly. They were trapped.

16

Return to Danger

Sarah checked her run as the two pikemen came forward to bar their way. 'Leave them to me, Sarah,' yelled the Doctor. 'Just keep running!'

Sarah saw the first pikeman lunge. The Doctor dodged and suddenly the pikeman sailed through the air, landing with a crash that knocked him cold. Sarah ran for the gate, and the second pikeman ran out. The Doctor grabbed him, twisted and threw, sending the man flying after his fellow. By the time Irongron and the others reached the yard, the dazed sentries were picking themselves up, and the Doctor and Sarah had disappeared into the forest.

At Sir Edward's castle, they were greeted like returning heroes, and plied with food, wine and questions. The Doctor explained what had happened as best he could. 'I think it's one of the most active days I've had for some time. Not as if I was a lad any more. Once you're over two hundred, you know . . .'

Sir Edward and Lady Eleanor took this calmly enough. They knew that wizards were more or less immortal. Sarah gave the Doctor a quizzical look, unsure as usual whether he was teasing or utterly serious.

'I fear your plans have miscarrried, Doctor,' said Sir Edward. 'What will you do now?'

'Wait till it's getting dark, and then go back,' said the Doctor cheerfully. 'The potion should be working by then.'

'Doctor, you can't go back,' protested Sarah.

'I've got to. Rubeish and all the kidnapped scientists are still there, remember. Linx is almost ready for blast-off—and when he goes Irongron's castle goes too.'

Lady Eleanor was struggling to understand. 'Irongron's castle is to be destroyed by sorcery? Then surely all is well. Why risk your life yet again?'

'There are innocent prisoners still inside, my lady. And I don't like to think of anyone going up in smoke, not even Irongron's gang.'

Lady Eleanor shook her head, clearly at a loss to understand such a soft-hearted attitude.

'All right, Doctor,' said Sarah resignedly. 'But if you're going back, I'm going with you.'

Hal spoke from his usual place by the doorway. 'I too will come with you, if my lord permits.'

The Doctor smiled. 'Thank you, both of you. I'll need all the help I can get.'

Rubeish sat slumped in the corner, concealed amongst the other kidnapped scientists. Like the rest of them, he was pretending to be in an exhausted coma. But he took every opportunity to study Linx and his activities through his home-made spectacles.

The Sontaran had been very busy since his return to the workshop. The last of the work was finished now, and all the equipment had been re-installed in the ship. Linx had disappeared inside some time ago. Through the open door Rubeish could see him moving busily around a tiny control room. A fierce white light blazed from the ship and there was a sudden roar of power that shook the workshop. It settled down to a steady throbbing, and Linx came out of the ship. Rubeish let his head slump as the Sontaran walked across and surveyed the slaves he no longer needed. 'Thank you, my friends,' he said ironically. 'Your work is finished. Now you may rest, until the power build-up is complete. After that, your troubles will be over!' He turned and went up the stairs.

Once he was safely away, there was a low babble of speculation amongst the scientists. Rubeish looked across at the throbbing ship. 'I think you'd better get a move on, Doctor,' he said to himself. 'I've a nasty feeling time is running out!'

The Doctor stepped out of the TARDIS and closed the door behind him. Over his arm was something that looked like a furled umbrella, though it was silver rather than black. He touched a control in the handle and the umbrella sprang unfurled. He touched another control and it closed itself up again. Satisfied, the Doctor hung the umbrella over his arm and strolled off through the forest, like a gentleman on his evening walk.

Sarah and Hal crouched in hiding at the edge of the forest, looking across at Irongron's gatehouse. They had seen the little serving wench come out with a pot of oatmeal, and the sentries eating their supper from wooden bowls. Sarah hoped Irongron was tucking into his stew, and wondered what Meg was making of the disappearance of her temporary helper. Suddenly she clutched Hal's arm. 'Look!' One of the sentries leaned against the wall, yawning hard. He slid slowly to a sitting position and his head slumped on his chest. Puzzled, the second sentry went to see what was the matter—and toppled to the ground beside him.

'Good evening,' said a polite voice. The Doctor was just behind them. He appeared to have changed his coat and shirt, and looked cool and elegant. Sarah couldn't help feeling a little envious. She'd changed back into her boy's clothes at Sir Edward's castle, and she didn't feel she was looking her best. She noticed the silver umbrella over the Doctor's arm. Surely he hadn't gone back to the TARDIS because he was worried about rain?

She pointed to the dozing sentries. 'It's working, Doctor!'

'Aye,' said Hal softly, 'the villains sleep like babes.'

The Doctor nodded. 'We'll wait just a little longer. It'll be dark soon—then we'll go in.'

Rubeish looked up eagerly as they came down the cellar steps, though he was too crotchety to show how pleased he was to see them. 'Ah, so there you are at last, Doctor. Something most interesting happening down here.'

The Doctor looked worriedly at the throbbing spaceship. 'So I see. Where's Linx?'

'No idea. He got that thing going and cleared off.'

The Doctor looked round. 'And the osmic projector?'

Rubeish shrugged. 'He took everything back in the ship.'

'Then I'll just have to take it out again,' said the Doctor. 'Hal, scout around the castle and see if Irongron and the rest of the men are sleeping yet. If they are, disarm them and come back here.'

Hal nodded and went silently up the steps.

The Doctor headed for the open door of the scout ship. 'I must get that osmic projector.'

Sarah looked at the throbbing scout ship. It seemed alive with malignant power. 'Can you switch it off, Doctor?'

'I can try,' said the Doctor grimly. 'If I don't suc-

ceed, we've about ten minutes to evacuate this castle.'
He disappeared into the ship.

Hal stepped cautiously over a sleeping man-at-arms,
taking the man's sword as he passed by. Cautiously he
went on his way. He had already unlocked Irongron's
dungeon, sending an astonished squire Eric scurrying
into the forest. Now he was on his way to the great hall.

The Doctor popped out of the scout ship clutching the
osmic projector. Sarah nodded towards the still-throb-
bing ship. 'You couldn't shut it down then?'
    The Doctor shook his head. 'The drive unit is sealed
and locked, set for automatic count-down. Linx must
have taken the activator key.' He lugged the osmic projector to a nearby work-table, and made a number of
adjustments. The projector hummed with power and
projected a cone of bright light just in front of itself.
'Right, that should do it,' said the Doctor. 'Has to be
one at a time, I'm afraid. Shove the first one into the
light, will you, Professor?'
    Rubeish bustled a bemused scientist forward until he
stood in the centre of the light-cone. 'Better come over
here and see how it's done,' said the Doctor. 'I may need
you to take over.' Rubeish came to look over the Doctor's
shoulder. The Doctor pointed to three switches. 'Now
all you do is this, this and this—in *that* order. Got it?'
    The light-field grew brighter and the scientist simply
faded away. The Doctor chuckled. 'There! That'll surprise the Brigadier! Next, please.'
    Rubeish propelled another scientist into the cone of
light.

Irongron pushed away his half-empty platter and took a
swig of wine. Meg's stew seemed even worse than usual.

He looked up at Linx, his voice slurred and heavy. 'For the last time, good toad, let there be no more talk of leaving us.'

Squat and powerful, Linx seemed to dominate the room. 'I come to give you fair warning, Irongron, I am leaving. Our alliance is at an end.'

'It ends when I say it ends, toad-face, and not before.'

Linx turned away. 'You would be well advised to leave this castle, and capture another. Soon you will have need of it.'

Bloodaxe shook his head, trying to clear it of sudden drowsiness. 'He threatens us, Captain,' he said sluggishly.

Irongron clapped him on the shoulder. 'He does not understand our ways, good Bloodaxe.' He peered muzzily at the Sontaran. 'Tomorrow, Linx, we take Sir Edward's castle. Tonight, we feast. We attack at dawn.'

Linx gave one of his rare smiles. 'By your dawn, I shall be seven hundred million miles from here. Can I be concerned with the fate of primitives?' He turned and marched heavily from the hall.

Bloodaxe rubbed a hand across his eyes. 'What did he mean, Captain?'

Irongron shrugged. 'He is a toad at heart, Bloodaxe. Who knows what a toad thinks?'

'Truly said, Captain. Truly said.' Bloodaxe's head fell forward into his plate of stew.

Irongron yawned. 'This stew has made me heavy!' He noticed that the guard by the door was already asleep—and reached for a plate to throw at him, but suddenly the effort seemed too great . . . He yawned again, and slumped forward on to the table.

One by one the osmic projector had beamed the kidnapped scientists back to the twentieth century. There were three more to go . . . The cellar door opened with a crash. Linx was at the top of the stairs, ray-gun in hand.

17

Linx's Departure

The Doctor snatched up his silver umbrella. 'I'll keep him busy,' he shouted. 'You two send off the rest of them.'

Linx came slowly down the steps, his eyes flaring red at the sight of the Doctor. He raised the ray-gun—and the Doctor flicked open his umbrella. The red glare crackled around the umbrella. But the Doctor was safe, unharmed behind the deflecting shield of the metallic foil.

There followed a strange and deadly game of hide and seek. Linx edged slowly around the Doctor, trying to get a clear shot at him. The Doctor dodged about in front of Linx, keeping the umbrella-shield between them. Linx leaped to one side and fired—but the Doctor leaped too, whipping up his shield. The deadly game went on.

Meanwhile Rubeish had despatched another scientist, and another . . . and another. When the last one had disappeared Sarah said briskly, 'Now you, Professor.'

Rubeish peered short-sightedly at her. 'Well, really, I think I ought to stay and help the Doctor.'

'Off you go,' said Sarah firmly. She shoved him into the cone of light. 'Now then—this, this and this, wasn't it?'

Rubeish was still chatting away. 'Well, goodbye, young lady, and good luck. It really has been a most fascinating . . .' Still talking, he disappeared.

Sarah turned her attention back to Linx and the Doctor. They were stalking each other around the workshop, the Doctor swinging his silvery shield to deflect the blasts from the ray-gun.

Suddenly the nature of the struggle changed. Linx feinted, dodged to one side, then sprang forward with incredible speed. His arm swept out, smashing the flimsy shield from the Doctor's hand, leaving the Doctor defenceless. Linx stood gloating for a moment, raised his ray-gun—and the Doctor smashed it from his hand with a precisely-timed kick. For a moment they confronted each other. The lipless mouth of the Sontaran stretched wide in a fearsome grin, and his little eyes glowed red with bloodlust. Slowly he began shuffling towards the Doctor.

The Doctor backed away. He was facing an opponent too heavy to throw, too strong to hold, too tough to be disabled by any blow. Unless, unless he could get behind him, and strike at the probic vent . . .

Well aware of the Doctor's intentions, Linx made sure to keep his front to his enemy. Twice the Doctor tried to get round behind him, but the menace of Linx's slashing blows kept him back. The Doctor knew that if just one of those blows landed he would be in trouble. And if Linx ever got him in his grip . . . They shuffled round and round the workshop in a deadly waltz, jockeying for position.

Hal slipped cautiously into the great hall. Irongron and Bloodaxe were snoring at the table, sleeping men-at-arms all round them. Hal slipped from one man to another, taking knives, swords and crossbows and tossing them out of the window. He disarmed Bloodaxe, then turned to Irongron, the last, and the most dangerous.

Hal reached for Irongron's sword and began sliding it from its sheath—and Irongron's eyes came open. Perhaps it was because he was so much stronger than the others, perhaps because he'd eaten less of the stew—whatever the reason, Irongron was suddenly awake. With a roar he surged to his feet, smashing Hal to the ground with a single blow. He looked muzzily around at his sleeping men. 'Treachery,' he muttered thickly. 'Black sorcery! That toad Linx has bewitched us all.' Drawing his sword he staggered from the hall.

Sarah looked desperately round the workshop. If she could find some weapon, perhaps she could strike Linx down as Rubeish had done. Before she could act, the Doctor's foot slipped, and Linx was upon him. A smashing blow sent the Doctor flying across the cellar. He scrambled to his feet and backed away, but the blow had weakened him. Instantly Linx was upon him again. He seized the Doctor by the arm, and hurled him across the room. The Doctor cannoned against a wall, and almost fell. He shook his head half stunned and backed away. Linx sprang forward again, and grappled with him. The Doctor put forth all his strength and actually succeeded in holding Linx for a moment. The two stood straining, motionless, locked together like some statue. Then Linx hurled the Doctor to the ground. The Doctor struggled to rise and then collapsed.

As Linx went to pick up his ray-gun from beneath the bench, Sarah threw herself upon him but he brushed her casually away. She flew across the room, slammed into a column, and fell.

Linx picked up his gun, took careful aim at the Doctor—and the door crashed open. Irongron stood swaying at the top of the steps. He glared at the glowing scout ship. 'Destroy my castle by sorcery, would you, toad-face? Irongron is too strong for your magic.' Raising his broadsword, Irongron moved down the steps. 'Die, star warrior!' Linx raised his ray-gun and gave Irongron one long blast, the weapon at maximum power. Irongron twisted in the grip of the red glow, then crashed down the steps like a falling tree.

As Linx turned to shoot down the Doctor and Sarah, an urgent bleeping note came from the control room of his ship. He remembered that he had left the ship on automatic countdown. Now there was not so much as a second to spare. Besides, his enemies would die in the blast . . . Linx snatched up the osmic projector, ran into the control room and took his place in the flight-chair. His stubby fingers flew over the complex controls. The throbbing of the ship rose higher and higher until the castle was shaken to its foundations . . .

Hal shook his head and staggered to his feet. The whole room was shaking crazily. He lurched across to Bloodaxe and slapped his face. Bloodaxe's eyes came open. He stared dazedly at Hal and reached for his vanished sword. Hal shook him savagely. 'Listen, dog! In minutes now this castle will be destroyed by sorcery. If you'd save your miserable skins, rouse your knaves and get you gone.' Hal snatched up his longbow and ran from the room.

Bloodaxe looked round. The room was vibrating, and great cracks were appearing in the walls. A dull roaring filled the air. Bloodaxe ran about the room, kicking his men awake. 'Flee, dogs,' he yelled. 'Flee for your lives!' The dazed men-at-arms began stumbling to their feet.

Sarah struggled desperately to get the Doctor on his feet. He was still half-stunned and she was badly shaken by her own fall. 'Doctor, do get up,' she begged. 'We've got to get out of here.' At last the Doctor managed to stand up and Sarah helped him to stagger up the stairs.

Suddenly Hal appeared at the top of the steps . . . Through the open door of the scout ship, he saw Linx in his command chair, and instinctively seized the chance for a last blow at the enemy. Swiftly he fitted an arrow to his bow and loosed it at the half-seen figure behind the already closing door. It was the shot of his life. The arrow took Linx directly in the probic vent, and he slumped forward over the control panel. He was already dead when his hand stabbed down on the firing button.

In the workshop the roar of the scout ship motors rose to a shattering howl. 'He's hit the take-off button,' yelled the Doctor. 'We've got less than a minute to get out of here.'

Somehow they staggered up the steps, through the corridors, across the courtyard and out of the castle. The roar of the ship's engines was deafening now. Sarah was dimly aware of some of Irongron's men running past them, but she scarcely noticed them. Her one thought was to get the Doctor away from the castle in time. Hal beside them, they stumbled on through the dark forest, trying to put as much distance between them and the doomed castle as they could. At last Sarah collapsed. 'I can't go on any further . . .'

As usual the Doctor was recovering with amazing speed. 'It's all right, Sarah,' he said. 'This is far enough.'

They turned and looked behind them. Irongron's castle was just visible through the trees. There was a sudden brightness, a blinding flash of light, and a shattering explosion. With an eerie howling sound a glowing fireball rose over the trees and disappeared into the night sky.

Commander Linx was going back to his war at last.

*

The Doctor paused by the open door of the TARDIS and shook hands with Hal. 'You can tell Sir Edward his troubles are over, Irongron, his castle, his magic weapons *and* his sorcerer—all destroyed.'

'Will you not tell him yourself, Doctor?' pleaded Hal. 'He will reward you richly. We owe you much.'

'I'm sorry, Hal, but we must go now. Mustn't we, Sarah?'

Sarah nodded. 'I'm afraid so. Goodbye Hal.'

'Goodbye Sarah.' Hal stepped back, raising his bow in salute. 'Goodbye, Doctor. You are truly a great magician.'

The Doctor smiled. 'Nonsense, Hal. As a matter of fact, I'm not a magician at all.'

Sarah looked thoughtfully at him, remembering all that had happened since they first met. 'I'm not so sure about that, Doctor!'

The Doctor bustled her into the TARDIS and closed the door behind them.

Hal watched quite unsurprised as the blue box faded away with a wheezing, groaning noise. How else should a wizard depart? He turned and looked behind him. The fiery red glow from the blazing ruins of Irongron's castle was lighting up the night sky. Hal turned away and began his journey home.